PERFECT MATCH: KING'S CHOSEN

PERFECT MATCH SERIES

I. T. LUCAS

King's Chosen

When Lisa's nutty friends get her a gift certificate to *Perfect Match Virtual Fantasy Studios*, she has no intentions of using it. But since the only way to get a refund is if no partner can be found for her, she makes sure to request a fantasy so girly and over the top that no sane guy will pick it up.

Except, someone does.

Warning: This fantasy contains a hot, domineering crown prince, sweet insta-love, steamy love scenes painted with light shades of gray, a wedding, and a HEA in both the virtual and real worlds.

Intended for mature audience.

---

*L*isa eyed the large blue envelope. "Thank you. You guys are the best."

If it was a gift certificate, which it probably was, Lisa hoped it was to a department store. Getting older meant that it was time to start taking better care of her skin, and good moisturizers were pricey.

"You're welcome." Bridget thrust it into Lisa's hands. "Now open it already."

The gleam in Bridget's eyes didn't bode well for something as mundane as a department store gift card.

Unfortunately, her besties weren't into practical gifts.

What had they gotten her? A gift certificate to an adult toy store? A ticket to a male strip show?

Ann lifted her Margarita in a salute. "A quarter of a century is a milestone birthday, and we decided to splurge on something special for you." She waggled her brows.

"Thanks a lot. Way to make me feel ancient."

Ann shrugged. "It's just a number."

Turning the envelope around, Lisa searched for clues. If it was something embarrassing, she would just stick it in her purse and open it when she got home.

Charlotte, who was bristling with excitement, waved an impatient hand. "Open it already."

"Do I have to?"

"Absolutely."

At least it wasn't a box or a gift bag. That precluded something like the vibrator they had gotten Linda for her birthday. But if it was a gift certificate for a private male striptease like the one they'd gotten Rachel, she was just going to thank them, put it away, and forget about it. It was a waste, but gifting it to someone else was out of the question.

Lisa wasn't as nuts as her friends. They were the best, but they constantly pushed her limits. To be frank, though, she needed that.

The seven of them had started the birthday tradition in college. Everyone would pitch in for the gift, and the idea that got most votes won. Obviously, Lisa's never had. According to her friends, her ideas were no fun.

That's what happened when an accounting major shared an apartment with a bunch of art and theater majors. Practical had never been part of their vocabulary, and every little thing led to a drama. Nevertheless, she wouldn't have traded any of them for someone else, and not only because they made her seem less boring by association.

Sharon, Rachel, and Bridget had moved out of their shared rental house years ago, but Lisa, Charlotte, Ann, and Linda were still there. The only difference was that each had her own room now. With the insane cost of housing in Santa Monica, moving out of a rent-controlled house would have been foolish, and for once her financial acumen had not been ignored.

New rents had doubled over the last seven years.

Taking a deep breath, Lisa tore the envelope open and pulled out a cream-colored card. The title "Perfect Match" was embossed on one side, and there was a web address and an access code on the other. That was it. No instructions, no brochure to explain what the heck it was. Nothing.

Except, the name said it all.

"Do you guys really think that I'm so desperate that I need a matchmaking service?"

True, she hadn't had a boyfriend in forever, but it wasn't as if she was sitting home alone, eating ice cream and watching the dumb box.

Not every day, anyway.

Lisa had been on plenty of dates. The problem was that all of those guys had been meh, and her impressive list of first dates had translated into a very few seconds and almost no thirds.

Perhaps the problem was that most of those dates had been arranged by her well-meaning friends, and it was quite obvious that Lisa didn't share their taste in guys.

Ann giggled. "It's not that kind of matchmaking service."

"What is it then?"

From across the table, Charlotte smirked. "They promise to find you a perfect sexual match and then arrange a virtual hookup."

Horrified, Lisa glanced around the busy restaurant, but it didn't seem as if anyone had heard Charlotte's explanation. "Keep it down. And are you guys nuts? You know me better than that. I don't do hookups."

Her friend leaned closer and whispered. Loudly. "Yeah, and that's what so great about this service. A virtual hookup is not the same as a real one. None of your many prudish objections apply. You can't catch a disease, there is no morning-after walk of shame, and you don't even have to wax."

True. Except, having sex with a stranger, even virtually, wasn't Lisa's thing. She wanted romance, she wanted intimacy, and she wanted love.

Was that too much to ask for?

Charlotte kept going. "It's new. They've been beta-testing

3

it for over a year and only opened it officially a couple of months ago, but there is a waiting list already. I put your name down as soon as I heard about it. It's perfect for you."

Lisa shook her head. Out of all the crazy ideas her friends had come up with, that one took the gold medal. "Please explain how it works, and what am I supposed to do with it. I'm not saying I will, but just out of curiosity."

Bridget crossed her arms over her chest. "Don't you dare waste it. We spent a fortune on this, and it's nonrefundable. Not unless you go through it and then claim you were unhappy with it and ask for your money back. There is a satisfaction guaranteed clause."

At least, there was that. She could pretend to do it and then ask for a refund. "Okay, I'm listening."

"So it goes like this," Charlotte started. "You fill out a questionnaire. It asks you about your perfect type of guy, your sexual fantasies, and that sort of stuff. It's supposedly very thorough. The computer compiles the data and matches it against what it has collected from guys who filled out the same thing. It finds you the perfect match, schedules an appointment for both of you at the same time, but you don't get to see each other. You get hooked up to a virtual machine in one room, and the guy in another. The machines could be in the same facility or across the globe, and you wouldn't know. You get to experience your craziest sexual fantasy in complete anonymity."

Lisa chuckled. "I can just imagine the kinds of guys who purchase the services. Perverts, geeks, old men... you get the picture. "

"What do you care?" Charlotte waved a dismissive hand. "All you see is the avatar the guy creates for himself, and he's sure going to look like a hunk. This is totally cerebral, and, personally, I think it's beautiful. Freedom from body issues, insecurities, hang-ups, social conventions, etc. You can be whoever you want to be and do whatever with whomever."

"What if it turns out gross and I want out?"

"There are safeguards. A certain word you can use that freezes the program. It's all on their website. You can read it all online. Any question you can imagine is answered."

"I'm sure I can think of a few new ones. Like, what if I like the guy and want to meet him? Not that it's a possibility, but hypothetically."

"You can put in a request, and if the guy agrees, information can be exchanged, like email addresses or phone numbers. And the other way around. But they don't recommend it, precisely because of what you said before. There might be a huge age difference, or he might be on another continent. Currently, they only have the two offices in the States—one is in Los Angeles and the other one in New York, but they plan on opening branches in the UK, Canada and Australia."

"Another possibility is that he is married," Ann said.

"The perfect way to cheat on one's spouse without actually cheating. Does virtual sex count as infidelity?" Lisa wasn't sure.

"I don't think so," Ann said. "It's like watching porn with a twist. Although I don't think I would be okay with my boyfriend doing that."

"Just think of the possibilities." Charlotte lifted her hands in the air. "It's a great way to experiment. If I want to check out sex with another chick, I don't think Ron would mind."

"Pfft." Ann crossed her arms over her chest. "Knowing your pervy boyfriend, he would want to watch. But would you allow him to do the same with another guy?"

"Sure. It's not real. It's a fantasy, so why not?"

Thinking of it objectively, it really was just a step beyond porn, and supposedly everyone was doing it.

Except for Lisa. "I wonder if I can request to be paired with single guys only."

Linda shook her head. "A single man can still have a girlfriend or lie on the questionnaire. It's not like they are doing background checks for virtual hookups, which is another reason not to meet the guy face to face. He can be an ax murderer for all you know."

"Stop analyzing this to death." Charlotte clapped Lisa on the back. "You're looking to be matched with someone who'll fulfill your most secret, filthiest fantasies, not a future husband. When was the last time you had sex? And I mean a good one. Memorable. "

Never.

Lisa had had a total of two steady boyfriends, and neither had been particularly memorable in that department. And as for her numerous dates, none had inspired even a tiny spark of desire, let alone hopping in bed and doing the horizontal mambo.

It was pathetic.

There was only one man she'd ever felt physically attracted to, like in weak in the knees attracted, and he barely acknowledged her existence.

Lisa didn't even know his name.

They worked in the same building and shared an elevator ride from time to time. Sometimes he would nod at her, and she would smile back.

That was the extent of their contact.

He looked to be in his mid-thirties, had smart eyes, and filled his fancy business suits very nicely. He also smelled fantastic. She hadn't seen a wedding ring on his finger, but that didn't mean he wasn't married. No way a man like him hadn't been snatched up a long time ago. He probably had kids too.

Her attraction to the mystery guy baffled her. Lisa had met guys who were just as good-looking or more, but none had had the same effect on her. There was something about him, some inner strength that she found enticing. And it didn't matter that he never smiled, never acknowledged anyone's presence even though he'd been riding the elevators with the same people day in and day out.

Perhaps it was the suit. Or the slight nod she was the only recipient of.

Maybe she had a weakness for men in suits. Or maybe it was his severe demeanor. It should've repelled her, but for some reason, it had the opposite effect.

Her office was on the third floor, and his was higher up. It seemed so easy to just stay in the elevator, ride it up to where he got out, follow him to his office, and find out his name. But she didn't have the guts to do it. Even though he'd never done more than nod in greeting, he must've noticed that she'd always gotten out before him. There was no reason for her to go any farther than that.

Her intentions would've been transparent.

inally, some peace and quiet.

With a sigh, Samuel leaned back in his chair and looked out the windows of his twelfth-floor corner office. The sun had set hours ago, and since the smog was not too bad the stars were visible.

Not that Sam was into stargazing, but he needed to take a moment to wind down before tackling the stack of proposals he had to go over. His cyber security business was booming, which was good, but he was running out of steam, which was bad.

At least now that everyone had gone home, Sam could concentrate on the task without being bothered by phone calls and people coming in and out of his office. Or so he thought until Gregg opened the door and walked in, his flip-flops slapping against the floor.

As usual, his partner's idea of appropriate office attire was baggy shorts, a button down shirt that was never ironed, and either sandals or flip-flops.

Gregg planted his butt in a chair across from Sam. "Why are you still here?"

"I can ask you the same question."

"I forgot something in my office. What's your excuse?"

"I have work to finish."

"Don't we all. Go home, Sam. "

"What for? So I can take the proposals home and finish going over them there? I prefer not to. It's not like I have someone waiting for me."

"And whose fault is that?"

"Fuck off, Gregg. I'm not in the mood for one of your philosophical lectures."

"Not all women are nasty, self-centered, manipulative, gold-diggers."

No, just the ones Sam had had the misfortune of dating.

He was done with that.

Maybe he should get himself a mail-order bride from Ukraine, or some other shit-hole that happened to produce hotties who wanted American husbands. But with his luck, he'd get stuck with another nasty viper. The only difference would be the Russian accent. Or Ukrainian. Was there a difference?

"You know what your problem is?" Gregg stretched his legs out and crossed his arms over his chest.

"No. But I'm sure you're gonna tell me."

"You have a weakness for the glitzy model types. Why do you think they put so much effort into their looks? It's a bait to lure horny guys like you. You should look for a nice, ordinary girl."

As if that was going to happen while Sam worked hundred-hour weeks and interacted socially only during charity events, which were also work-related.

In the world of big business, Samuel was the face of the cyber security firm that he and Gregg had founded a decade ago. Participating in those events was not optional, and it wasn't fun. Supposedly, their purpose was to raise support for charity, but for him, as well as for many of the other attendees, the main purpose was drumming up new business.

Mingling and schmoozing with the CEOs and decision makers of big corporations meant connecting with potential new clients.

That was where he'd met Alexandra. Or rather where she'd first sunk her claws into him. And before her, it had been Natasha, and before that, Tiffany.

They could've been clones. Beautiful, elegant, charming, attentive, and single-mindedly dedicated to achieving one goal—snagging a wealthy husband.

With each one, Sam had hoped this time it would be different. After all, some of the women attending those events were CEOs of companies and top-tier executives, but he'd never been lucky enough to be approached by one of them. The ones who gravitated toward him had only one thing in mind, and contrary to their sales pitch, it wasn't sex, it was matrimony.

As the saying went, lunacy was doing the same thing over and over and expecting different results. Since the last breakup, Sam was doing his damnedest to ignore attractive women in general. He was tired of the drama, and he needed a break to clear his head.

It wasn't easy. Temptation was everywhere. Like that pretty accountant in the elevator, with her glasses and her sensible shoes and her guileless eyes. It was all fake. Underneath the unassuming, nice girl façade there was probably just another viper. After all, she was a junior partner in a large CPA firm, which meant that she was smart, calculating, and interested in money.

A nice girl. Right. Not in his world. Maybe they existed in fairy tales.

"Don't you have anything better to do than harass me?" Sam glared at his partner. "I'm not sitting here and scratching my balls. I have work to do."

Gregg grinned. "Actually, I need to get back to my office and pick up one of those gift certificates the guys from

Perfect Match gave us. I'm going to take it home and schedule myself a virtual hookup."

"Have fun. Just remember that those gift certificates represent half of our compensation." The other half was in the company's stock.

The job they'd done for Perfect Match wasn't one of Sam's better deals. The company was young, and all their investment capital had gone into developing their sophisticated hardware and software. In addition, it had been a cyber security nightmare that had taken months to implement. The main reason Sam had agreed to take it on at that price was that the CEO was an old buddy of his and Gregg's from Caltech.

Besides, he believed the company had promise, and if it succeeded, their stock would one day be worth a lot more. Not only that, in the long run they would become a well-paying client. With plans to expand their services globally, they would need a lot more cyber protection and Sam's company would be the natural choice.

Given the glowing reviews of the beta testers, the service had great potential. Especially once they reached a volume that would allow them to lower their prices. Currently, it was out of reach for most.

"Oh, I will." Gregg waggled his brows.

"You really enjoyed the test run."

When they'd been approached, Gregg had volunteered to check it out before they committed to a complicated job that initially wasn't going to bring in any money.

"It was all they'd promised and more. You should try it."

"I will, just after you tell me all the details of your fun-ride." Which wasn't going to happen. Gregg, who had no problem butting into Sam's love life, was very tight-lipped about his own. Real or virtual.

"Let me tell you one thing, Sam. Women are just as horny as men. Perhaps more so because they have better imaginations. Give a woman a safe environment to explore her sexuality, and she'll blow your mind." With that, Gregg pushed to his feet, pulled out a folded envelope and dropped it on the desk. "Here, your perfect, custom-made girlfriend awaits."

Sam arched a brow. "I thought you forgot to pick up the gift certificate and that's why you were back."

"I did. I forgot to pick one up for you. That one was mine."

3

Did you hear from them yet? Lisa read the text message from Bridget, the same one she'd been sending her every morning for the past week.

Not yet. Once I do, you'll be the first one to know.

I'd better be. I'll text you tomorrow.

"Was it Bridget?" Charlotte put her coffee mug down.

"Yeah. Same question as yesterday and the day before. It said on the company's website that it would take them between one and four weeks to find my perfect match."

"It has been a week."

Lisa shrugged. "They still have three more to go."

"I hope it won't take that long. We are all dying of curiosity. My birthday is coming up next, and I'm going to start throwing hints that this is what I want, but first I need to hear from you if it's worth it."

"Provided they find me a match."

"They will." Charlotte walked to the sink and rinsed out her mug. "I'm off to work. I'll see you later."

"Have a great day."

Smirking, Lisa lifted her mug and took a sip. If no match could be found for her, she'd get a refund.

She was banking on that. In fact, the way she'd answered the hundreds of multiple choice questions, she'd practically guaranteed no sane guy would want any part in it. Basically, she'd let her girly imagination run wild, and there was no way any guy would match that.

It wasn't that she'd purposely lied on the questionnaire, just that the type of guy she'd described didn't exist outside of fairy tales. Kinky ones. Well, kinky by Lisa's prudish standards. Her friends would've laughed at what she considered unconventional.

Only three more weeks to go, and she'd get a refund and forget all about that stressful episode.

For what her crazy friends had paid for that service, she could buy Lancôme's entire line of moisturizers and facial creams.

Before heading out the door, Lisa checked her hair and applied some lipgloss. In case she ran into her mystery man on the way to her office, she needed to look at least decently put together. Not that she expected to get anything more than a nod, but it would make her feel better to know that she didn't look frumpy.

As Lisa parked in the office building's underground and headed toward the elevators, she glanced around, hoping to spot the object of her fascination. Curiosity had her wondering what model car he drove. Knowing that would give her some insight into his personality.

Was it a sexy Porsche, or a stately Mercedes?

It wasn't that Lisa was impressed by money or expensive cars, but judging by his expensive suits, her guy wouldn't be driving a Honda.

Or maybe he had a driver?

That would explain why in the three years she'd been working in the building she'd never seen him in the parking garage, only in the elevator.

Three years, wow. That was a long time to pine for a stranger.

She should grow a set and approach him.

Right, as if she would ever have the courage to do that. A guy like that would probably laugh his ass off if a girl like her propositioned him.

With those unsettling thoughts running through her mind, Lisa was almost afraid to see him walk into the elevator. She was going to blush for sure and give herself away.

Thankfully, he didn't.

Lisa should've felt relieved, not disappointed.

At her desk, she booted up her computer and checked her emails. Most were from clients, others were from stores following her around on the net, but only one made her heart skip a beat.

Lisa got up, walked to her office door, locked it, and then went back to sit at her desk. For a few moments, she just stared at the screen, afraid to click the email open. There was no way someone had picked up her fantasy.

Shit. What was she going to do now?

Because if someone had, she would actually have to do the things she'd put on that damn questionnaire, and she was too much of a chicken to do so even in a virtual world where no one knew who she really was.

"Okay, Lisa. He's not going to jump out of the screen at you and tear your clothes off. Just read it."

Visualizing that made her chuckle, releasing some of the tension. Mouse hovering over the email for a couple more seconds, she forced herself to click it quickly before courage deserted her.

Dear Ms. Montgomery,
Congratulations.

A perfect match was found for you. Please confirm the date and time of the appointment by clicking the link below.

After all that mental preparation, the email was underwhelming. But then what had she expected? Details? A script?

For an accountant, she had a very vivid imagination. Releasing a breath, she looked at the date again.

Damn, Saturday was only two days from now, and she had no good excuse for rescheduling the appointment. Besides, it was allowed only once. If she couldn't make it the second time either, the money would be forfeit.

Better to get it done sooner than later. Less time to stress and obsess.

With a shaky hand, Lisa pressed the confirmation link.

A moment later another email came in.

Dear Ms. Montgomery,

Thank you for confirming the appointment. Please make sure to arrive on time.

Wearing comfortable clothing is recommended.

Okay, so no Spanx and no pantyhose.

---

4

*A*t two o'clock on Saturday, Lisa arrived at A Perfect Match offices, wearing a loose T-shirt, yoga pants, and flip-flops. It didn't get more comfortable than that unless she took the bra off. But there was no way she was showing up in public without one. Her breasts were nice and firm, but her nipples tended to react to the slightest drop in temperature. An air-conditioned space was all it took to get them stiff and pointy.

"Good afternoon, Ms. Montgomery." A pleasant-looking young woman welcomed her with a smile. "I'm Sarah." She offered her hand.

"Hi." Lisa shook it.

Thank God it's a woman. She would've died of embarrassment if the technician was a man.

"I assume that you've read all the instructions and explanations, but before I hook you up, I want to go over the major points and see if you have any more questions."

"Sure. But first I need to know if you've tried it." Getting instructions from someone who'd never done it wasn't going to cut it.

The girl giggled. "Of course I did. All of us working here

have done it many times. We were part of the beta team who helped tweak the program."

Lisa released a relieved breath. The tech's admission made her more comfortable to ask her questions. "Did you enjoy it?"

"It's addictive. But I'm enjoying it more now that there is a larger pool of people. Before, I was scared of sharing the experience with one of my coworkers. We were all looking at each other, searching for clues." She rolled her eyes. "Talk about awkward."

Sarah's honesty and openness about her experience made Lisa more comfortable. "I can see how it could be embarrassing. I wouldn't want my coworkers to even know I'm doing this, let alone chance to have one of them as my virtual partner."

Unbidden, the handsome face of her elevator crush popped into her head. She wouldn't mind sharing the fantasy with him, but then she would have to quit her job and move to another city because she would die of mortification if he suspected it was her.

"Yeah. But there were also plenty of volunteers. So no one knew for sure. But enough about me. Let's go over what you should expect."

"Shoot."

"First of all, just like in a dream, the perception of time is misleading. You may experience virtual days or even weeks in the span of the three hours you're allotted."

Lisa nodded.

"Everything will feel real. Your brain cannot distinguish between artificial neural input and reality. Some of it will even manifest physically."

"I understand."

"There are safeguards built into the program. You can't die. If your stress levels reach a certain threshold, the program will shut down immediately. You also have a safe

18

word to freeze it, but even if you forget it, and that can happen when you're totally immersed in the virtual universe, the monitors will detect signs of distress and freeze the program for you. You can override the freeze by simply saying 'continue.' Any questions?"

About a thousand, but none that Lisa could articulate. "I don't know. What do people usually ask?"

"Will they remember it. Yes, you will. Another common question is whether your partner will be able to recognize you on the street. The answer is that it depends on the avatar you choose and the way you describe your ideal man. The software combines the two inputs and creates an avatar your partner finds desirable and that you're comfortable with. The more the avatar looks like you, the better the experience because it feels more real. But it's up to you. Before the program begins, you'll be presented with your avatar, and you'll get to choose which features you want to change. You can decide to keep your eye color but change your nose. Make your breasts larger, your legs longer, slimmer waistline. Those are the most common ones for women. Guys want to be taller, more muscular, and better endowed. A few want a stronger jawline, but that about sums it up for men. Women tend to go for a whole makeover."

Lisa smiled. "That part I'm actually excited about."

"Why? Aren't you excited about finding your perfect match?"

"To tell you the truth, I'm terrified. According to your website, I'm not going to remember who I am in my real life, and a whole new backstory is going to be uploaded into my brain. I'll think of myself as a different person living in a different world."

"But that's the fun part. Fantasy at its best. And when you wake up, it's going to be exactly the same as waking up from a dream. You'll be back in your real life. But unlike most dreams, you're going to remember everything from the virtual experience as well."

"It still scares the crap out of me."

Sarah frowned. "You may need a mild relaxant."

"Don't mind if I do. But I don't want it to make me loopy or diminish the experience for me."

Was it her talking? She sounded as if she was excited.

"No problem. I'll give you something very mild only for the first half an hour. After that, I'll check your stress levels. If you're doing okay, I won't give you any more."

"Sounds good to me."

"Let me hook you up and check your vitals." Sarah pushed to her feet and motioned for Lisa to follow her into the adjoining room.

A theater-style recliner occupied the center of the room, with an ominous-looking helmet thing the size of a salon hair dryer hovering above it. An assortment of wires stretched from the helmet to a big rectangular console behind the chair. The rest looked like what one would expect to find in a hospital room.

It didn't look sexy at all, but maybe that was why Lisa was breathing easier. Or maybe it was Sarah, with her honesty and friendly attitude.

"If you need to go to the bathroom, now is the time," Sarah said.

"Good idea."

"Over there." The tech motioned to the only other door besides the one they'd entered through.

When Lisa came back, Sarah motioned to the chair. "Take a seat."

Taking a deep breath, Lisa got on the contraption, which was much more comfortable than it looked.

"Tell me your avatar's name, again."

Oh, God, here it goes. "Princess Annabel."

When Lisa was a little girl, she'd dreamt about being a

princess. She still thought it would be cool to play one, and the name Annabel sounded so much more exciting than plain old Lisa.

What she wondered, though, was what kind of a guy fantasized about playing the part of her prince?

5

*A*nnabel mixed a tiny drop of black paint into the green, dipped her brush in it, and applied another stroke to her landscape. The meadow below was breathtaking, the grass so vividly green that she was having a hard time matching the color.

The view from the top of the hill was well worth the long climb, including hauling up her easel and all her other art supplies. Not that Annabel had carried any of that. But she'd felt sorry for poor Mary. By the time they'd crested the hill, her maid had been huffing and puffing. Annabel had sent her back to rest and come back later with a lunch basket. At least that was the excuse she'd given the girl. As much as she liked her, Mary was way too chatty, and her prattling wasn't conducive to Annabel's creativity.

Alone with the breathtaking nature, with nothing to disturb the serenity and magnificence of the setting, Annabel did her best work.

Except, her reprieve hadn't lasted nearly as long as she'd hoped for. She could hear someone climbing up the hill, and by the familiar huffing and puffing, it was Mary back with the picnic basket.

It wasn't time for lunch yet, was it?

Sometimes, while absorbed in her painting, Annabel lost track of time.

She turned around just as Mary finished the arduous climb. Given the sheen of sweat on her forehead and her rosy cheeks, the girl must've run all the way up.

"My lady," she said breathlessly as soon as her head crested the hill.

"What's wrong, Mary?"

"The Prince." Mary bent down, placing her hands on her thighs. "He is on his way. He wouldn't listen to anyone. The chief advisor sent me up to warn you. He is delaying the prince as much as he can."

A prince? Which one? There were dozens of them.

Their corner of the world was comprised of many small to mid-sized monarchies, and one big one—Algenia—the superpower that shielded them all from other superpowers.

The small monarchies didn't need to keep an army, just an honor guard for their monarchs and a small police force. The downside of the arrangement was that half of the taxes collected went to Algenia as payment for their protection. All in all, not a bad deal. Keeping an independent army would've cost just as much if not more.

"Which one is he?"

Mary looked at her with wide eyes. "The Prince. Prince Thorsten."

Oh, shit.

Annabel looked down at her simple dress and the paint-splattered apron she'd put over it. She'd come up here to paint, not expecting any visitors, and certainly not the bloody Crown Prince of Algenia.

A fine time he'd chosen to show up.

It must've been a deliberate move on his part to catch her alone. Her parents, her brother Norman—the crown prince of their small monarchy—and his pregnant wife Muriel were all visiting Muriel's parents.

Annabel had been left in charge. Normally not a problem since the council was running most things anyway. Except, she could've used her parents and brother as a shield from Thorsten.

Annabel knew precisely what had pissed him off enough to make him travel all the way from Algenia's capital to her hill. Only, she hadn't expected it to matter to him so much. In any case, she was going to play it dumb and pretend that she had no idea why he was paying her a visit, while at the same time softening him up with her gracious hosting.

"It's okay, Mary," she said while removing the soiled apron and tossing it aside. "Go back down and have Cook prepare a picnic basket for two. Find the finest bottle of wine and put it in there. Also, a blanket or two to sit on and maybe a couple of pillows."

Mary wrung her hands. "But, my lady, the prince is on his way, and I can't leave you alone with him. It's unseemly."

The girl was absolutely right. But if Thorsten had come to yell at her, Annabel didn't want witnesses. "Don't worry about impropriety, Mary. The prince and I are childhood friends. I have nothing to fear from him."

If only she believed it…

As a boy, Thorsten had been a bit too cocky, but he'd also been easy to smile and fun to be with. Except, he'd grown up into a harsh and merciless man. Or at least that was what she'd heard. They hadn't seen each other in years.

Mary curtsied. "As you wish, my lady. I'll be as quick as I can."

Please don't.

"I want the picnic to be worthy of the prince, Mary. Rushing Cook is only going to stress her out, and she's going to burn something. Let her do things at her own pace."

Mary curtsied again. "Yes, my lady." Lifting her skirts, she scurried downhill at a trot.

"Be careful!" Annabel yelled after her.

Silly girl was going to sprain an ankle, or worse.

Nervous butterflies taking flight in her belly, Annabel smoothed her hand over her hair, hoping there weren't too many flyaways. She'd put it in a simple braid to keep it away from her face, and it wasn't the most flattering hairdo for her.

She remembered that Thorsten had liked her hair loose around her shoulders and spilling down her back, but she'd been a little girl then, not a grown woman who was supposed to take greater care with her appearance.

Oh, well. It was too late to do anything about it now. Besides, she didn't have a comb or a mirror to fix herself up.

A few moments later, Thorsten's head crested the hill, and his expression was just as pissed off as she'd expected. What she hadn't anticipated, though, was how incredibly handsome he'd become.

The years had been kind to her childhood crush.

She curtsied. "Hello, your Highness. What a pleasant surprise. What brings you to our modest monarchy?"

"Drop the pretense, Annabel. You know exactly why I'm here. Why didn't you answer the summons? Each and every one of the princesses did, even those who are not of age yet. All except you."

Lowering her eyes, she curtsied again. "I meant no offense, your Highness. I'm truly sorry if my lack of response was construed as such. The truth is that I didn't think of myself as worthy of such an honor. The future queen of Algenia should be someone more refined and sophisticated than simple me." Or want the position, which Annabel most definitely did not, her childhood infatuation with the crown prince notwithstanding.

The last time she'd spent time with Thorsten, he was

fifteen and treated her like a little sister, and she was ten and had a huge crush on him.

But a lot had changed over the past nine years. Thorsten's older sister had abdicated her title as crown princess, and Thorsten had been forced to take over. Preparing for his new role had superseded all of his prior personal interests and friendships, and since then everything he had done was as the Crown Prince of Algenia.

The Thorsten she'd known had ceased to exist.

Annabel had changed too. She wasn't a naive young girl anymore, infatuated with an older boy who, for some inexplicable reason, had shown some mild interest in his best friend's little sister.

Besides, the only reason Thorsten was looking for a bride was his mother's health. The queen wished to step down in favor of her son, but the law demanded that he marry and produce an heir first.

Annabel didn't want to be anyone's broodmare.

In fact, she didn't want to marry at all. Her older brother was the crown prince of their tiny monarchy, and therefore his wife had come to live with him in the palace. Annabel would have to move to her future husband's court, and she didn't want to do that. She loved her country. Leaving it and her family would be heartbreaking. If being a spinster was the price she had to pay for staying in the home she loved, Annabel was more than willing to do so.

The worst possible future was marrying Thorsten. Not only because the boy she'd fancied had turned into a harsh man with a reputation of a brute, but because playing queen of Algenia, with all of its court politics and intrigue, was her personal definition of hell.

"What's wrong with you, Annabel? Every girl in all the known monarchies dreams of becoming the future queen of Algenia."

"I don't." She lifted her chin. "Therefore, I must be addleminded and unsuitable for the position." That was actually not a bad strategy.

She should've thought of it earlier and made sure to spread rumors about her eccentricity. They wouldn't have been a lie either. Everyone thought she was weird for refusing suitors and remaining single at nineteen.

Thorsten shook his head. "You were always smart. Too smart for your own good. Even at ten, you were never caught without a witty comeback."

It was a polite way to put it. Others thought that her outspoken attitude was rude or even flippant.

Annabel waved her hand as if he'd just proven her point. "Not something you want from your future queen."

"On the contrary." He sat down on a boulder, his muscular thighs bulging as he spread them wide to keep his balance. "Come over here, Annabel." He patted his thigh.

Had he lost his mind? Expecting her to sit on his knee? She wasn't ten years old anymore.

Crossing her arms over her chest, Annabel lifted her chin. "I will do no such thing."

The smile slid off Thorsten's handsome face, replaced by a stern expression that was frightening but at the same time oddly arousing. "When I tell you to do something, Annabel, I expect you to obey immediately and without question."

That should've angered her, not aroused her.

Damn, what is wrong with me? Why is Thorsten's brutish arrogance making me tingle in all the wrong places?

The power in his commanding voice had affected her in the strangest way. It must've addled her brain because she felt compelled to do as the prince had commanded. Baffled, Annabel took a couple of steps toward him, but she then shook her head to break the spell he must've cast over her and stopped.

She wasn't some blushing chambermaid to be ordered by the prince. She was a princess. "You forget, your Highness,

27

that I'm not one of your subjects. There is no law that says I have to obey you."

His smile was chillingly wicked. "Oh, but there is. As my future wife, you are my subject."

In a swift move that caught her completely by surprise, Thorsten reached for her hand and pulled, upending her over his outstretched knees.

"What the hell do you think you're doing?" Annabel shrieked, pushing with all her might against his thigh to get off him.

"What I've been craving to do for the past nine years." He pushed her back down and lifted her skirts, exposing her naked behind.

She thrashed harder. "Stop it, you brute, let me up."

"Only after I punish you for ignoring the summons and insulting me." He smacked her upturned behind. "My country." Another smack. "And my mother, the queen of Algenia."

Thinking that was it, Annabel pushed up again. But he wasn't nearly done. As a volley of smacks landed on her naked bottom, she was stunned into silence.

Thorsten wasn't hurting her, not really. She knew he could do much worse and was merely toying with her, but the entire episode was surreal. And strangely arousing...

She remained outstretched over his knees even after he'd stopped and had begun caressing the barely there sting away.

In a raspy voice that betrayed his own arousal, Thorsten whispered, "You have the most beautiful bottom I've ever had the pleasure of spanking."

That statement had her up in an instant. For some reason, Thorsten's hand on her bottom bothered her much less than than the thought of his hand on another woman's backside.

She didn't get far, though. He held on to her hand and pulled her back to sit on his lap, just as he'd intended from the start. Annabel wanted to protest, but he wrapped his arms around her and shut her up by kissing the living daylights out of her.

All rational thought was obliterated by the onslaught of sensations. Thorsten's lips were soft and yet firm, his tongue coaxing and insistent at the same time, his large hands on her back warm and strong.

God, he was setting her on fire.

"What are you doing to me?" she murmured as he let her come up for air.

"Convincing you to be my wife."

She chuckled. "That's a very strange way to go about it. Most men bring flowers. You spanked me."

He kissed her nose. "Because, my dear Annabel, I knew that you would enjoy that more than flowers."

"I did not." Yes, she did. But she wasn't going to admit it. Never.

And what was more, how could he have known that when she herself hadn't?

"We will discuss the consequences of lying at a later time." Thorsten assumed his stern demeanor again, but there was laughter in his eyes.

"Oh, yeah? What do you have in mind?"

He didn't have a chance to answer because of the heavy huffing and puffing that announced Mary and another maid's approach. Lifting her off his lap, Thorsten straightened her rumpled skirt.

A moment later, Mary and Ida climbed to the top of the hill, hauling between them a huge picnic basket.

---

6

*B*eautiful, witty, and feisty.

Thorsten had adored Annabel as a little girl. As a woman, she was everything he could've ever wanted in a wife and more.

The best part was that she didn't want him. As strange as it seemed, her refusal had lifted a weight off his chest.

When his mother had announced her intention to step down, forcing him to choose a wife, the first and only woman that had come to his mind was Annabel.

Every day since the summons had been issued to all eligible princesses and high-born ladies, requesting them to submit their candidacy, he'd been waiting to get Annabel's. And with each passing day that it hadn't arrived his ire had risen.

It had been a blatant show of disrespect, but he knew it hadn't been her parents' doing. The king and queen of Mondera would have never dared to risk alienating their protector and the most powerful monarchy in the region.

The angrier he'd become, the more he'd suspected it was a ploy to get his attention. Just another form of manipulation. He was so sick of it. The length to which some of those princesses and their families had gone in order to gain his favor or at least get his attention had been astounding.

But Annabel truly didn't want to be queen.

Which meant that if he succeeded in winning her over, it would be as Thorsten the man and not Thorsten the future king of Algenia.

After the two young maids put down the heavy basket, which was the size of a travel trunk, Annabel untied the bundle that was strapped to the taller one's back, and together they spread a thick woolen blanket over the ground. Two sizable pillows went on top to make sitting more comfortable.

Watching Annabel help the maids reinforced Thorsten's impression of her. She wasn't a spoiled princess who was content to be served. Not that he would allow her to do such things when she was his queen. There were liberties a princess could take but a queen couldn't.

After that was done, the maids started pulling one dish after the other from the basket and arranging everything on the blanket as nicely as they could.

There was enough food there to feed a troop of soldiers. Thorsten hoped his guard was taken care of, and that accommodations had been found for them in the barracks. Rushing to see Annabel, he hadn't stuck around to check.

"Thank you." Annabel knelt on the blanket, rearranged her skirts around her legs, and sat down.

The maids took a few steps back, looking lost as to what to do next. Shifting from foot to foot and wringing their hands, they waited for their lady's instructions.

"That will be all, thank you. You can go back." Annabel waved her hand, shooing them off.

"But, my lady… " one of them started.

"You heard the princess. Do as you're told," he barked at them.

31

Blushing, the one who'd spoken stammered, "Yes, your Highness. I'm so sorry, your Highness."

They both curtsied and scampered away.

Annabel narrowed her eyes at him. "Are you always so rude to the help?"

Thorsten reached for the platter of grilled chicken, cut the bird down the middle, and loaded Annabel's plate first and then his. "They shouldn't question your commands. Perhaps in your case it's not as crucial, but imagine me in the same position. What kind of a ruler would I be if my servants answered my demands with a 'but'? Or imagine my soldiers questioning my orders."

After a moment of mulling it over, she nodded. "You're right. I apologize. You and I live by very different rules."

"Not for long." He winked.

"About that. I really would make a lousy queen, Thorsten. I hate court politics. I hate stuck-up people. I hate smiling when I don't feel like it. And I hate being the center of attention."

"So do I. So what?"

"Since when? As I remember, you love being the center of attention."

"Granted, I don't mind that. But I hate all the rest. Therefore, I don't smile when I don't feel like it, and as soon as I'm crowned, I'm going to get rid of all the conniving, manipulative vermin infesting my court."

Annabel looked at him with horror in her eyes. "Are you going to kill them all?"

Damn it. The rumors that vermin had been spreading about him painted Thorsten in very unflattering colors. "No, I'm not going to kill them. Kicking them out of the palace grounds will do. Don't believe all the nasty rumors they've been spreading about me."

He often wondered about their agenda. What purpose did it serve to make him appear as a brute?

If they thought his sister would reconsider, they were wrong. Granted, Amelia was a much more amiable and pleasant person than he was, and they probably thought she would be easier to manipulate, but that was precisely the reason she'd abdicated. The official reason was her wishing to wed a wealthy merchant and not a prince, but their mother had been more than willing to amend that law for her, allowing Amelia to marry her chosen. His sister insisted that the law remain in effect.

She simply didn't want to rule, and frankly, he couldn't fault her for that. If they had a third sibling, Thorsten would have gladly foisted the succession on him or her.

Looking down at her plate, Annabel cut a piece out of the chicken. "Some of the rumors are true," she murmured.

"Which ones?"

To avoid looking at him, she cut another piece. "That you're a brute with women."

He chuckled. "I haven't heard any complaints."

Finally, she lifted her head and pinned him with a hard stare. "You're the crown prince, Thorsten. Of course, no one would dare complain."

Frustrated to no end, Thorsten ran his fingers through his hair. People were so quick to believe the worst of him. But he'd thought Annabel was smarter than that.

"There is only so much a woman can fake. Some responses can't be manufactured, and they tell the truth."

He would've said more, but Annabel seemed so innocent. She probably had no idea about what went on between a man and a woman in bed.

"You spanked me. That's brutish."

"You call that a spanking? It was a patting. Does your bottom even sting?"

She wiggled, and he wondered if the cause was discomfort or arousal.

"Not anymore. But it was humiliating."

"You were aroused."

Averting her eyes didn't help hide the crimson blush that spread over her porcelain skin. She neither confirmed nor denied, choosing to say nothing. She would make a fine diplomat.

"Don't be embarrassed, sweetheart. It's natural."

"No, it's not."

Sweet, naive Annabel. There was so much more he could teach her. Thorsten was looking forward to many delightful educational nights.

7

*A*nnabel shook her head. It couldn't have been the stupid spanking that had aroused her. There was no way it could've had such an effect on her. Being touched by Thorsten had done it. She was a grown woman, and what had been a young girl's infatuation had turned into a physical attraction. His hand had touched her naked bottom, the first male hand to ever touch her intimately. No wonder she'd reacted like that.

"I know what I'm talking about, Annabel. I'm not a novice at this."

"I bet." She could just imagine how many women he'd been with.

He must've heard the sarcasm in her tone. "Those days are over. From now on, you are the only one for me."

As if she was going to believe that. Fidelity among royalty wasn't common. Her brother seemed wholly devoted to his wife, but he might be the exception. She refused to even think about her own parents. Hopefully, they were an exception too.

"You assume too much, your Highness. I didn't agree to be your wife."

Thorsten's expression darkened, and before she realized his intentions, he lifted her up and pulled her onto his lap.

Too close.

Touching him, smelling him, feeling his hands on her, it was all too much. "Let me go," she breathed, her voice sounding unconvincing even to herself.

"Tell me you feel nothing for me, and I will. But if you lie, I'm going to spank you again, and this time I'll make sure the sting lasts."

Damn.

As her breath caught in her throat and her traitorous nipples hardened, she couldn't help but glance down at Thorsten's big hand on her thigh and imagine it cupping her breast. A wave of desire washed over her, making her dizzy. Feeling faint, she swayed in his lap.

What was he doing to her? Why was he affecting her like that?

Thorsten adjusted his grip, stabilizing her. "I'm waiting."

"I had a crush on you when I was ten. What I feel is probably echoes of that." It wasn't a lie, but it wasn't the entire truth either.

Thorsten's other hand roamed over her back. "You're clever, Annabel. But I know you better than you think I do."

She turned in his arms and looked at his smiling eyes. So cocky, so sure of himself. "Tell me what you think you know about me."

"You're beautiful, and smart, and feisty. I know that you like to read a lot and to paint. I know that you're curious by nature, and I know that you're kind. I knew all of that before I came here. What I needed to find out, though, was if you're power and status hungry like the others. Which you're not. And also if you're passionate. I intend to be faithful to my wife, which means I'm not going to marry someone who's cold to me."

"And what's your verdict?"

His grin was so broad that his face must have hurt. "Oh, you're passionate alright. But I still need to run a few more tests."

Was he suggesting what she thought he was?

"I'm not going to let a man who's not my husband touch me."

"How about your fiancé?"

Annabel shook her head. With him so close, she couldn't think straight, and the way he kept pushing and cornering her, she wasn't going to manage one coherent thought.

"I need to think. You swept down on me like a thunderstorm, scrambling my brain and confusing me with the liberties you've taken. I need a few moments to breathe."

Resting his hand possessively on her upper thigh, he had his long fingers dangerously close to where she ached the most. "I'll give you more than a few moments. I'll give you until nightfall. But before I do, I want to make a few things clear."

That should be interesting.

She nodded.

"The reasons you had for refusing me are no longer relevant. I'm not the monster rumors painted me to be, and I'll make sure that your queenly duties will be limited to what you're comfortable with. I need a wife first and a queen second. I know you have some feelings for me because you admitted it yourself, which is more than you'll have for any other jackass who will come courting. You're a logical woman, and you must realize that I'm the best choice for you. The only thing that is holding you back is fear."

He wasn't wrong.

Thorsten was like a force of nature. Of course she was terrified of giving him so much power over her. But maybe she could negotiate with him while he was still willing to make concessions. Being a princess, Annabel had learned a thing or two about power plays.

"I'll make a deal with you," she said hesitantly. He might take offense to her trying to negotiate the terms before even agreeing to marry him, and she might end up over his knee again—bottom up.

Surprising her, he smiled. "By all means."

"If I agree to marry you, and I'm not saying that I will, I want you to grant me the freedom to visit my family as often as I wish."

"Agreed. But unless we visit them together, I don't want you gone for more than one night."

"That's reasonable."

"What else?"

"I need you to promise me to always treat me with respect. In public and in private."

He frowned. "That's a given."

Apparently, they had very different ideas of what constituted respect. "I need you to promise that you'll never spank me again."

He shook his head. "No. Next."

"Why not? It's disrespectful to me."

"No, it's not. It turns you on, and I plan on doing it often. But in private."

Damn, stubborn man. Just as she thought she was making progress with him and was starting to consider him seriously.

"That's not what turned me on. I had a huge crush on you as a kid. Now that I'm a woman, touching you, smelling you, feeling your hands on me, that was what stirred something in me. Not your display of brutishness."

His hand glided up, his fingers so close to the moist place between her legs that she could almost feel them. "I'll make you a deal of my own. Tonight, when I come to your bedroom, we're going to test your theory."

"You can't come to my bedroom!"

"I can do whatever I want. If you're concerned about your

reputation, get rid of your maids and make sure no one disturbs us."

For a moment, Annabel didn't have a response. The truth was that she could fume and fuss, and still, Thorsten would do as he pleased. No one was going to stand in the way of the Crown Prince of Algenia. But would he stoop as low as forcing her?

"I can't believe you would do that," she whispered.

She knew the exact moment her meaning dawned on him. The hand on her thigh tightened painfully. "What kind of a man do you think I am?"

He looked scary, but that didn't mean she was going to let him off the hook. "The kind who does whatever he wants."

His fingers on her thigh loosened their grip and Thorsten sighed. "I didn't mean it like that. I'm so used to issuing orders that I no longer know how to talk any other way. My intention is to seduce you, and I know you're going to let me because you want me as much as I want you. But if you say no, I'll respect it."

Annabel lifted a brow. "No questions asked?" she teased, repeating his own words.

"No questions asked. I'll treat a no from you as a command to be immediately obeyed."

"Every no?"

"Each and every one."

"What if I say no to attending court?"

"Then it's a no. I'll make up an excuse for you."

"But you didn't listen when I told you to put me down."

"You didn't say the magic word."

"Please?"

"No. The magic word is no. Plain and simple."

Hmm. Those were terms Annabel could accept.

8

*A*s Thorsten neared the barracks, he forced the stupid grin off his face. The commander of his personal guard hadn't been happy about him going to see Annabel without an escort, but that hadn't been the first time they'd argued about Thorsten's solo excursions.

Crown prince or not, Thorsten refused to give up his freedom. The compromise they'd reached was a commoner's garb and a hooded cloak to hide his face, which was overkill. His facial features weren't all that unique, and although he was tall, his height wasn't unusual. Without the princely attire, Thorsten was indistinguishable from many other young men.

Unless someone paid close attention, the plain clothing was usually enough to hide who he was. What he needed to be careful about, however, was his attitude.

As long as Thorsten slouched his shoulders, walked with a slight shuffle, and didn't do much talking, no one paid him special attention. That was how he could spend many an evening in the local taverns, listening to people talk and learning first hand what troubled his subjects. It was invaluable information that he had no other way of obtaining. His advisers told him what they wanted him to hear, and he never completely trusted his mother's spies and who else they were reporting to.

The disguise also worked great for visiting ladies who weren't part of his court.

Thorsten had made a point to avoid those vipers. His rejection must've rankled, and he suspected they were the source of the nasty rumors about him. Especially the ones about him being a brute with women.

"My prince." The commander bowed as Thorsten entered the barracks. "Would you like to inspect the accommodations?"

"I trust you took care of everything, Thomas. You can give me an update while we train."

"Certainly, my prince." Thomas bowed again. "I'll get our gear."

"Were there enough bunks for everyone?" Thorsten asked once Thomas returned and they stepped outside.

"Half of Mondera's so-called army is accompanying the royal family on their visit to the in-laws, so there was plenty of room for our men." Thomas cast him a sidelong glance. "How did it go with the princess?"

Now that they were out of the soldiers' earshot, there was no longer need for formality, and Thorsten could talk freely with his old friend. "Splendidly."

"Why didn't she answer the summons? Was there someone else?"

That was what Thorsten had been afraid of and what had brought him galloping to her tiny monarchy in person. Finding out the real reason was one of the happiest moments of his life.

He smirked. "The lovely Annabel doesn't want to be a queen."

Stopping mid-stride, Thomas turned to him. "And you believed her? She's manipulating you, my friend. I haven't

41

met a girl yet who doesn't dream of becoming the next queen of Algenia."

"Not Annabel." Thorsten kept walking. "She hates court politics, which I empathize with wholeheartedly, and the idea of being the center of attention terrifies her."

Thomas shook his head. "I might have believed it before the ball. I've never known women could be so vicious to each other. But apparently, when the prize is the crown prince, all bets are off."

"They are of no consequence. The only one I ever wanted was Annabel."

"What about Rowenia? She assumes you are hers for the taking."

The mention of that name had the small hairs on the back of Thorsten's neck stand to attention. He wasn't afraid of any man or an army, but that woman scared him.

Before meeting her in person, he'd assumed that the nasty rumors about the Crown Princess of Deluvia were the same as the ones about him, an attempt to tarnish her reputation by those opposing her future rule. But now he was inclined to believe that the woman was indeed a witch.

No wonder Rowenia had assumed that she was the winner in the competition for Thorsten's affections, and that he was going to choose her as his queen.

She was beautiful, almost unnaturally so, stately and confident, but she was also condescending and cruel. He'd seen the way she'd treated the staff, and yet, once she'd entered the ballroom, he'd felt compelled to spend the rest of the evening with her.

But as much pressure as she'd put on him to announce her as his betrothed, he'd had no trouble resisting her bewitchment. All he had to do was to think of Annabel's beautiful face and get furious at her for not showing up.

Hopefully, Rowenia got the message and found some

other prince to sink her claws into. If not, there would be hell to pay once he announced Annabel as his fiancé.

Deluvia was a powerful monarchy with a strong army, and Rowenia's father had probably been hoping for an alliance of marriage with Algenia. Spurning his daughter might entice him to seek consolidation of power in a different manner. He might go to war or seek an alliance with a different superpower.

All in all, it would've been most beneficial for Algenia if Thorsten had chosen Rowenia. But not for him. Annabel was the one dream he wasn't willing to sacrifice for his country. But even if Annabel refused him, he wouldn't wed the Crown Princess of Deluvia. She was bad news.

"I wouldn't wed Rowenia even if she were the only princess available. The woman is nasty."

"And dangerous."

Thorsten's lips thinned in determination. "When the time comes, I'll deal with the threat she represents. First, I have to woo the one I want. Annabel is not mine yet."

Thomas grinned. "I wish you best of luck, my friend. I'm just glad you haven't fallen under the evil witch's spell."

9

*A*fter soaking in a bath full of soothing aromatic salts for more than an hour, Annabel should've been relaxed. Instead, her hands shook as she tried to braid her long hair.

Thorsten loved it loose, but if she didn't braid it first, it was going to be fuzzy and stick out in all directions.

"Let me, my lady," Mary offered.

Annabel was about to refuse but then thought better of it. Mary liked to gossip while brushing her hair, and she could give her updates about Thorsten, and what he'd been up to since they'd parted at the bottom of the hill.

"Here you go." She handed her the brush. "Was Prince Thorsten satisfied with his accommodations?"

"Oh, yes." Mary gently brushed the long strands. "He said they were adequate and ordered a bath to be drawn for him. But he didn't retire to his rooms right away. He and the commander of his personal guard sparred in the practice yard."

"Sparred? Not fenced?"

"They did that too, but first they sparred." Mary fanned

herself with her hand. "When they took their shirts off, the other maids and I swooned. They are both so handsome."

With a frown, Annabel glanced up at Mary's reflection in the mirror. "They were showing off for the staff?"

Thorsten was about to be king. Taking his shirt off in front of a bunch of maids was undignified. It irked her to think of them lusting after her man.

Mary rolled her eyes. "They didn't know we were watching them. We were taking turns peeking through the second-floor window, but then stupid Ida had to giggle and give us away. I almost withered and died when the prince looked up and frowned at us. He is so scary when he's angry." Mary smirked. "But still no less enticing."

"You shouldn't have been peeking at them when they obviously wanted privacy."

Mary giggled. "I'm sorry, my lady. We won't do it again."

Right. And cows would sprout wings and fly.

"Make sure to tell the others that Prince Thorsten is off limits. They can gawk at the commander and the soldiers, but not at the prince. You don't want him to catch you doing that again. He might demand punishment to be meted out for your insolence." *And because he's mine.*

Mary's smile vanished. "Yes, my lady."

When her maid tied the ribbon to secure the braid, Annabel turned around and smiled at her. "Thank you, Mary. You have the rest of the evening off. Go visit your parents. You can stay the night and come back tomorrow."

For a moment, it seemed like the girl was about to argue, but then she closed her mouth and nodded. Maybe because she remembered Thorsten's scolding, or perhaps because she was eager to visit her family.

"Thank you, my lady." The girl curtsied and left.

Alone at last, Annabel went over to the window and sat on the bench to watch the sun go down. As soon as it was dark, Thorsten was going to come, and she wasn't going to say no.

To anything.

Not because she suddenly wanted to be queen, she still hated the idea, but because she craved Thorsten the brute. He could deny it all he wanted, but the fact remained that the future king of Algenia wasn't a gentleman.

The thing was, Annabel doubted a gentleman would've set her body on fire like Thorsten had.

As a princess, Annabel had led a sheltered, boring life, and the only adventures she'd experienced had been in the stories she'd read.

Thorsten was her chance of an adventure. She had no doubt that life with him would be a wild ride—far more exciting than anything she could've imagined as a wife of some minor princeling. Which was what lay in her future if she refused Thorsten.

Marrying for love was a fantasy a princess couldn't indulge in, but where there was lust, love could one day follow.

Undeniably, the one thing she and Thorsten had in abundance was lust.

10

*W*hen night fell, Annabel's heart began racing. What would Thorsten do to her? What would he demand?

Somewhere in the back of her mind, there was a vague impression that she wasn't a complete novice at this. Perhaps she'd dreamt about having been intimate with a man. But if she had, the dream must not have been very memorable because she couldn't bring up any details.

Naturally, Annabel wasn't ignorant on the subject of sex. It wasn't in her nature to remain in the dark about anything. She'd read, and she'd asked questions, embarrassing the hell out of Cook, who she had caught on more than one occasion necking in the kitchen with her husband of more than twenty years.

Lucky woman.

That was what Annabel wanted. Love and passion so strong and so deep that they withstood two decades of marriage and five children. To have that, she would give up her title and don a cook's apron.

A light knock on the door pulled Annabel from her reveries. Thorsten would've just barged in, she thought, so it couldn't have been him. Hopefully, it wasn't Mary or one of the other maids deciding to check on her.

Padding barefoot to the door, she opened it a crack.

"Are you alone?" Thorsten whispered.

Her eyes widened at the sight of him. "Yes."

He slipped in and closed the door carefully behind him, then turned the key to lock it. "One of your maids is dusting the paintings on the far end of the corridor. I barely made it without her seeing me."

That was so sweet of him. She hadn't expected Thorsten to make an effort to keep their rendezvous a secret.

"I forgot about Lorna. I gave Mary and Ida the evening off."

"You did?" He seemed surprised.

She dipped her head. "As per your instructions, your Highness."

His smile reminded her of a wolf's. "Suddenly you're so agreeable. I like it."

As he pulled her to him and kissed her, Annabel wrapped her arms around his neck and let herself melt into his hard body.

Deepening the kiss, Thorsten ran his hands down her back and cupped her ass, squeezing and holding her as he pressed his hard erection against her soft belly.

Through the thin fabrics of her nightgown and robe, she could feel it straining against his pants, becoming harder the longer he was kissing her.

"Do you ache?" she asked when he finally let go of her mouth so she could take a breath.

"Terribly."

When she put her hand on his chest, something wild and unfamiliar stirred inside her. Without further thought, she caressed the bulging muscles, following their contours down to the hard length she was so curious about.

As Annabel palmed him over the fabric, Thorsten sucked

in a breath and covered her hand with his, pressing it harder against his manhood.

"I want to touch you without a barrier between us," Annabel heard herself say and almost fainted from embarrassment a split second later.

Was she possessed by the spirit of a lusty wench?

"I knew it. Fiery passion burns beneath that cool façade of yours." Thorsten lifted her in his arms and carried her to bed.

"What are you going to do to me?" The old Annabel found her voice.

"Pleasure you into oblivion and then ask you to marry me again." He pulled her robe off, then went for the straps holding her nightgown up.

"Wait. I'm not ready for this."

"Not ready for me to see your beauty?" He smoothed his hand over the bodice of her nightgown. "This thing is so sheer I can see your magnificent body as if you were naked already." His other hand trailed over her exposed calf. "But taking it off will allow me to touch your skin. No barriers."

It was only momentary cowardice.

She'd already made up her mind to let Thorsten do whatever he pleased to her, but there was a big difference between making a decision and acting on it. Evidently, Annabel wasn't as courageous as she thought she was.

Chewing on her lower lip, she gave him a slight nod.

"That's my girl."

Without taking his eyes off her, he pulled the straps down, going slow and exposing her inch by inch even though he was right about the sheerness of her gown. She was already as good as naked to his eyes, but he was giving her time, removing that last barrier as slowly as he could.

There was nothing brutish about the way he was treating her. Maybe a gentleman would have waited for them to be married first, but she doubted anyone would have handled her with such tender care.

Every touch felt like a caress, and every look was smoldering with lust but also with deep affection.

Or was it love?

Could Thorsten have loved her for all those years, waiting for her to grow up and turn into a woman?

Pushing a hand under her, he lifted her a little, and with a final tug tossed the nightgown on the floor. Looking at her, he whispered, "Absolute perfection."

As Annabel fought the instinctive urge to cover her breasts with one hand and her embarrassingly moist center with another, she forced herself to look into Thorsten's eyes.

His pupils were so dilated that they were more black than blue, with only a thin blue ring surrounding the big black disks. She liked the way he was looking at her, as if she was the most beautiful woman he'd ever seen.

It gave her the courage to ask for what she wanted. "It is your turn to disrobe, my prince. I wish to gaze upon the perfection of your physique."

"All in good time, my princess. Your pleasure comes first." He sat on the bed beside her.

His warm hand on her tummy, he leaned to take her lips in a soft kiss, and as he licked into her mouth, his hand moved upward, stopping at the underside of her breast.

With her already stiff and achy nipples reacting to his touch, getting even tighter, the need to feel his hands on them became so overwhelming that she whimpered into his mouth and arched her back in a silent plea.

"Are you hurting, my love? Do you need me to relieve the ache?" he breathed an inch away from her mouth.

"Yes."

"All you ever have to do is ask." His hand closed over one breast, and a moment later his other hand joined in, massaging and kneading its twin. "Is that what you need?"

Annabel shook her head. He'd relieved some of the ache, but she needed something more.

As his hands moved downward, cupping the undersides of her breasts, she wanted to protest, but then he started strumming her turgid peaks with his thumbs, teasing her with a promise of something, but she wasn't sure what.

"Is that it?" he whispered again, his eyes blazing with such intense passion it was frightening to behold.

Annabel squeezed her eyes shut.

"I guess it's not." She felt him lean closer, and a moment later his warm tongue swept over one achy nipple.

"More," she demanded.

"Of course, my love." His lips closed over the stiff nub, and he sucked it in.

The moan that escaped her throat was deep and guttural and very unladylike, but Annabel didn't care, especially since it seemed to please Thorsten.

Letting out a hum of approval, he murmured around her nipple, "That's more like it."

As his fingers closed around the other one and tugged in sync with the sucking, Annabel felt as if there was a coil inside her that was getting wound tighter and tighter the longer Thorsten played with her nipples. The sensation was an unfamiliar one, and she wondered what would happen when that coil sprung loose.

Would she explode?

A moment later she found out.

As he closed his teeth on one nipple and bit down gently, pinching the other at the same time, a scream erupted from some primal part of her, and if not for Thorsten surging up and covering her mouth with his, the entire palace would've known exactly what they'd been doing.

As he caressed her, mumbling incoherent endearments, Annabel allowed herself a few moments of floating on a cloud of bliss before coming back into her body.

Wow.

She opened her eyes and smiled. "Are you going to ask me to marry you now?"

If he did, she was going to say yes. Pleasuring her into oblivion had been a very persuasive tactic. As long as he promised to do that on a regular basis, she was willing to tolerate living in court with him.

"Not yet. I've just begun. "

"There is more?"

"Oh, sweetheart." He pushed a sweaty strand of hair away from her forehead. "There is so much more that it will take me a lifetime to show you everything."

"I'm not in a hurry."

11

*I*f his manhood weren't in such agony, Thorsten would have danced a victory dance.

Annabel was his.

God, he was so glad he'd followed his instincts and done everything he hadn't been supposed to. His gut must've known that an exceptional woman like Annabel required an extraordinary approach.

True, she wasn't so agreeable because she loved him, but because she craved what he could do to her. Still, it was infinitely preferable to her wanting him for his crown like all the others.

Love would come later. He would make sure of that.

The catch was that he needed to keep stringing her along and making her hunger for more. Which meant that he wouldn't be sinking his achy shaft into her soft wetness this time around.

Besides, he wanted Annabel to be a virgin on their wedding night.

Thorsten wanted to laugh at the absurdity of it.

He had a willing woman, and he was the one who was going to play hard to get so she would agree to marry him.

Absolutely, fucking, delightful.

He'd never expected a woman to marry him for his sexual prowess and not his crown. Hopefully, Annabel also liked him outside of the bedroom, at least a little. Good sex would make their marriage thrive, but more was needed to give it a solid foundation that would last for many years to come.

Which was another reason to take it slow. He needed to prove to her that he wasn't the brutish, heartless ruler the malicious rumors were painting him as.

"Are you going to take your clothes off now?" Annabel purred like a satisfied kitten.

"Not yet."

"Why not?"

"Because I'm not done convincing you to marry me. I want to make sure that you are never going to change your mind. And if I take my pants off, this will be over before it has begun."

"How about your shirt?" She eyed his chest hungrily.

"I can do that." He pulled the shirttails out of his pants, unbuttoned a few of the top buttons, and pulled the shirt over his head.

With Annabel's eyes following every move, he couldn't help but show off with some pectoral flexing.

"You're magnificent." Her gaze was appreciative and lustful. "You are very muscular. For a prince. "

"Just for a prince?" he teased.

"Well, I saw the blacksmith working shirtless once, and his were bigger."

Thorsten growled. "I'll have to challenge the bastard to a duel."

She laughed. "No, you won't. When you see him, you'll understand."

"Is he deformed?"

"No, but he is missing several teeth and has a face that scares children. He's a sweetheart, though."

Thorsten still wasn't happy. "Give me a straight answer, woman. Do you fancy the blacksmith or not?"

"I fancy only you." She smiled seductively. "Now come here and let me put my hands on you."

"That's the right answer."

Kicking off his boots, he pounced on top of her, the bed groaning and dipping from the added weight.

As Annabel spread her legs to cradle him between them, he had the dim impression that something wasn't right with that scenario. For a woman who'd never been with a man, she was far too comfortable with him in her bed.

But just as soon as that thought flitted through his mind, another one chased it off. Annabel was not like any other woman he'd ever known. He shouldn't expect anything about her to be conventional.

"I'm yours, sweetheart. Touch all you want." Propping himself on his forearms, his chest hovering only a few inches above hers, Thorsten waited for Annabel to start exploring.

With wonder in her eyes, she put her soft palms on his pectorals, then smoothed them over to his shoulders, his arms, his back. She seemed to be learning his body, memorizing every ridge and valley.

Her touch was more explorative than erotic, but it was the closest he'd ever felt to being loved by a woman. For lack of a better description, her touch was loving. Then she lifted her head and kissed him, her little tongue so polite as it licked the seam between his lips, asking permission to enter.

A sweet, lover's kiss.

At this rate, by the time he left Annabel's bedroom, Thorsten would be head over heels in love with her. He couldn't have asked for a better outcome—provided he was reading her right.

Taking over, his hand holding on to her slender nape, he deepened the kiss and ravished her mouth.

What he got in return was her total and complete surrender. Annabel seemed drunk with passion, her eyes hooded with desire, her body loose and pliable under his.

It was so tempting to push his pants down and enter her, especially since he was sure of his welcome.

But he was the Crown Prince of Algenia, and succumbing to a momentary weakness was not in his nature. Resolve and adherence to goals was an integral part of who he was.

Kissing his way down her body, he nipped at her ribs, licked at her navel, and then when he got to where he wanted to be, he kissed the top of her mound.

Annabel didn't protest. With a sigh, she spread her legs a little wider, giving him complete access.

Again, he had that flitting thought that things weren't right. An untouched virgin should've felt scandalized by what he was about to do, not welcomed him without a word of protest. And again as soon as it occurred to him, the thought was pushed out by another. Annabel was unlike any other woman. She was unique in every possible way.

Her neatly trimmed curls glistened with the evidence of her desire, and as he pressed a gentle kiss to those pink, puffy petals, her softest skin felt hot on his lips.

Ending the kiss, he parted her with his thumbs and blew air on the heated flesh, cooling it down a little before extending his tongue and lapping at her juices.

Delicious. All woman. All his.

"Oh, God, Thorsten… " She lifted up, impaling herself on his tongue.

His princess was greedy in the best possible way. Thorsten speared into her, penetrating her with his tongue, then replaced it with a finger and flicked his tongue over the center of her desire.

Her moan was one of pleasure mixed with agony. Not pain, his finger had slid effortlessly into her tight, wet heat, but of pleasure too intense to bear.

"Come for me, sweetheart," he rasped.

"I can't. It's too much." Clenching her buttocks, she lifted up and to the side in an effort to escape his tongue.

Trained by the best of courtesans, he knew that some women's center of desire was overly sensitive, and that too much stimulation could feel uncomfortable instead of pleasurable. Thorsten eased up a little, licking at the sides and avoiding direct contact.

It worked just as he'd expected.

Letting out a sigh, Annabel submitted to his ministrations, trusting him to take care of her.

"That's my girl." He pressed a soft kiss to her rosy petals.

*a*s Thorsten lifted her legs over his shoulders, spreading her wide, Annabel wondered how something so wicked could feel so good. If Thorsten promised to pleasure her like that every night for the rest of their lives, she would not only marry him but follow him to the ends of the earth.

In the recesses of her mind, she was bothered by how good he was at this. Obviously, he'd had a lot of practice. With whom, though? Had he loved any of the women he'd bedded? Who were they?

His court was probably filled with beautiful women vying for his attention, and it would only get worse when he became king. Could she tolerate being married to him while knowing that at any moment temptation could lure him into the willing arms of another?

That was another reason Annabel didn't want to be queen. Every court had women looking to gain favor or influence or just boasting-rights for bedding the king. Even a decent man would eventually succumb to that much temptation.

A sharp slap on her butt cheek cut through that depressing line of thought like lightning.

She lifted her head and glared at Thorsten. "What was that for?"

"You were a thousand miles away. Stay with me, Annabel."

Letting her mind wander while he was selflessly pleasuring her must've hurt Thorsten's feelings. If the roles were reversed, she would've been offended too. Not to mention that those thoughts had cooled her fervor, which he must've noticed.

"I'm sorry," she murmured.

He kissed the stinging spot. "You're forgiven."

Making sure her mind couldn't drift again, he pushed a second thick finger into her tight, virgin sheath, stretching it almost painfully, and she wondered if he was still punishing her. But as he pulled those fingers out and then thrust them back in, again and again, the discomfort soon gave way to pleasure so intense that she could no longer think, just feel.

Thorsten didn't let up. With each passing moment, he intensified the onslaught on her sensitive, quivering flesh, thrusting into her with his fingers while rimming the center of her desire with his tongue.

With the coil inside her winding up tighter and tighter, Annabel's moans were getting throatier and louder. Seeking an anchor, she grabbed fistfuls of Thorsten's hair, and when his lips closed around her oversensitive nub, she pulled so hard it was a miracle the soft strands remained attached to his head.

Ignoring the assault, Thorsten groaned in pleasure and gently sucked the little nub in.

Her inner muscles convulsing around his fingers, and lightning exploding behind her closed lids, Annabel cried out.

Thorsten groaned again, the vibrations prolonging her climax.

When she could take it no more and pushed his head away, he let go, gently cupped her center with his hand, and came up to claim her mouth.

Annabel expected to be repulsed by her own taste on Thorsten's tongue, but she wasn't. In fact, the wickedness of it sent a new bolt of desire down to her core, when she should've been beyond spent.

It occurred to her that none of it came as a shock or even a surprise. Had she read about those sort of things in one of her books? Cook had certainly never mentioned anything as delightfully deviant.

Thorsten let go of her lips and looked down at her with a smug smile on his handsome face. Well, he deserved to be smug. What he'd done to her had been wonderful.

"Are you going to ask me to marry you now?" Annabel teased.

"If I do, what will be your answer?"

"You have to ask first."

His hand pressed harder against her wet center, and he pushed in with one finger. "You're mine."

Maybe. But she wasn't going to let him wring it out of her without asking.

"Ask, Thorsten."

Another finger joined the first, and she gasped, her eyelids fluttering shut for a moment. But she needed to see his face when he asked.

"Princess Annabel of Mondera." His fingers retreated and surged back. "Will you marry me, Thorsten, Crown Prince of Algenia?"

"Oh, oh, oh, yes I will."

13

When Thorsten left Annabel's bedchamber, it was after she'd passed out from the exhaustion of climaxing for the fourth time. He, on the other hand, could pound nails with the hard club pulsing painfully in his pants.

Leaving had been an exercise in willpower, but he didn't want the maid to enter Annabel's room in the morning and find him in her lady's bed. Annabel would never forgive him for tarnishing her reputation.

Back in his own room, Thorsten barely had the presence of mind to close the door behind him before digging the swollen member out from its confinement and squeezing it hard. Leaning against the door, he closed his eyes and pictured Annabel climaxing on his tongue. With a roar, he erupted on the third upward stroke.

But that only took the edge off.

It took two more full loads before his manhood was subdued into limpness.

Slumped against the door, he grimaced at the mess he'd made ejecting three full loads one after the other.

It wasn't something he could leave for his manservant or

one of Annabel's maids to clean. Which meant that the feared and powerful Crown Prince of Algenia had to take a towel, dip it in water, and wipe the floor, then wash his own soiled pants to the best of his ability, which wasn't impressive in the least.

His training hadn't included domestic chores. That was what servants were for.

Sleep eluded him for hours as he made plans for the hastiest wedding possible. The longer he mulled over it, though, the more apparent it became to him that there was no way to make a royal wedding happen in under a week. It would take months to prepare an event his mother would approve of, and probably Annabel too.

As much as she claimed disliking being the center of attention, he had no doubt her own wedding was the one exception.

Besides, he was the future King of Algenia, and it would be undignified for him to have a half-assed wedding ball.

The problem was that he couldn't wait that long, and yet he still wanted Annabel to be a virgin on their wedding night.

Hell, he didn't think she could wait that long either.

It was no longer about making sure she'd agree to wed him. Because he knew she would say yes. It was about doing things right so no one could ever claim there was a blemish on their marriage. If he were a commoner, Thorsten could have not cared less, but as a ruler, he had to live under different standards.

Luckily, it seemed that he'd managed to dodge the biggest sacrifice required of his station. He wasn't going to marry some heartless, cold princess like Rowenia, and spend his life wondering when she'd knife him in the back.

Thorsten smiled and palmed his erection again. He'd wanted a passionate wife, and as always he'd gotten what he wanted. Hell, he'd gotten way more than that. Annabel was lustful, incredibly responsive, and eager. Having her as his wife would make him the happiest man in all the known monarchies and beyond.

As he saw it, he had two problems to solve. The first was how to marry Annabel as soon as possible. The second was how to placate Rowenia and her father and avoid war.

Thorsten was still trying to solve the two puzzles as the first sun rays painted the horizon dark pink. Except, his eyes refused to remain open and he drifted off into sleep and into the oddest dream.

Walking into a tall, box-shaped building that looked like it was covered in mirrors, he proceeded to enter a rectangular carriage that took him and other passengers up, stopping at each of the many floors to let some out and some in.

For some reason, he expected Annabel to walk in. But the carriage kept going up and up, and floor after floor people got in and got out, but not his Annabel.

So how come he could smell her perfume in there?

Or feel her hand on his chest?

As Thorsten's eyes popped open, he clasped the delicate hand resting over his heart. Annabel was curled next to him, sleeping.

She'd come to him. His sweet Annabel had missed him.

As a wave of tenderness swept through Thorsten, he wrapped his arm around her, bringing her closer against his body, and leaned to kiss her forehead. That's how he should sleep from now on, with her by his side. Which left him with only one option. They were going to get married the same morning. The official ceremony and the big ball could come later.

14

*T*he moment Annabel woke up, she knew Thorsten wasn't there. Her bed, her room, everything felt empty and cold with him gone.

Without giving it a second thought, she pulled on her nightgown and her robe and then tiptoed to his room. She found him sleeping on his back, his face relaxed in his repose, his big body nude from the waist up.

Her man.

Thorsten, Crown Prince of Algenia, belonged to her—to keep and to hold for as long as they both shall live.

There was no point in keeping pretenses. From now on, she would always share his bed. Share his life.

Letting her robe flutter to the floor, she joined him. It felt so good and so right that she sighed and closed her eyes, putting her hand on his chest so he'd know who he belonged to even in his sleep.

Soft lips on her mouth woke her up.

"Good morning, my love," Thorsten whispered.

His love? He'd called her his love last night too, but that had been in the throes of passion.

Was it a figure of speech? A meaningless endearment?

The thing was, she could answer the same way and mean it. "Good morning to you too, my love."

Thorsten's grin was so broad that it split his face. In one swift move, he grabbed her by her waist and hoisted her on top of him.

She was looking down at the face of the man she loved, when he said it loud and clear, "I love you, my Annabel."

"As crazy as it sounds, I love you too, my Thorsten."

He frowned. "Why crazy?"

"Because we hardly know each other."

"We've known each other since we were kids. I loved you even then. And you loved me too. "

She rolled her eyes. "I was ten. I was infatuated with an older boy."

"I've been waiting for you to grow up."

She rested her cheek on his chest and sighed. "Yes, me too. But when you never came, and then the rumors about you started, I forced myself to stop fantasizing about you. It worked. I convinced myself that I didn't want you. "

He chuckled, the sound reverberating through his ribcage. "I'm glad that you changed your mind back."

"Me too. But we are not the same people we were then. And we don't know the new us."

"I disagree. Who we are on the inside didn't change much. We are older, and we have responsibilities that force us to act differently, but we are still the same. Besides, we have the rest of our lives to learn all there is to know about each other." He lifted her hand to his lips and kissed the inside of her palm. "I want us to get married today."

Annabel lifted her head. "I wish we could, but we can't. Our families will be furious. Especially yours. They need a big wedding with all the fanfare."

Thorsten's smile was conceited. "Didn't I tell you already that I can do whatever I want? We grab a priest, two witnesses, and get married. Then we will get married again in a big ceremony to make everyone else happy."

Playing with the sparse hair on his chest, Annabel blushed as she said, "You don't need to marry me to bed me. I'm yours, Thorsten."

"I don't want us to skulk around like a couple of thieves. I want you in my bed every night, and every morning I want to wake up with you by my side." He wrapped his arms around her. "This is too good to let even one day go by without."

"You're right. Let's do it."

15

"What would your poor mother say, my lady?" The cook wrung her hands together. "It will break her poor heart. And what about your reputation? You can't elope like some village girl."

Annabel clasped the older woman's hands. "In a couple of months, Prince Thorsten and I will have a big wedding. But we are too much in love to wait for so long, so we are going to have a small private ceremony first. I'm sure you can understand what it's like to be in love. I cannot bear the thought of being without him even for a day."

Thorsten didn't see the need to explain himself to the cook, of all people, but she seemed important to Annabel. The woman was the first person she told about their upcoming nuptials, not the chief advisor.

He wrapped his arm around her shoulders. "And I feel the same about the princess. Now, tell me where I can find a priest."

The cook cast him a reproachful glance but then sighed. "I still remember what it's like to be so young and eager for each other. There is a priest in the village of course. Someone will have to go get him." She looked at Annabel. "Maybe a small donation to the church will persuade him to keep his silence about your private wedding until the big one?"

Fear of retribution should be enough of a deterrent, but Thorsten had no problem with making a contribution. "I will take care of that. I'll send one of my soldiers to get him."

Annabel put a hand on his arm. "That's not a good idea if we want to keep this a secret. People would wonder why you're fetching the priest and rumors would start."

"Perhaps we shouldn't keep it a secret, then."

She arched a brow. "Or we can wait the two months, and in the meantime, you can court me officially."

The cook nodded enthusiastically.

Thorsten turned Annabel to face him. "We will get married today, and let it be known. I intend on taking you with me to the palace when I leave, and I prefer people gossiping about our impromptu wedding than about our improper conduct."

For a long moment, she just looked into his eyes, and his gut clenched with unease. What if she changed her mind? Propriety was important to a princess, much more so than to a prince. It wasn't fair, but the world was not a fair place.

"I agree."

He let out a relieved breath. "I love you."

She smiled. "I love you too, and I want us to be married today, but I can't leave with you before my parents return."

"Not a problem. I'll send one of my men with a message, informing them of our marriage and requesting their prompt return."

Annabel lifted her hand and cupped his cheek. "Maybe we can wait with the ceremony until they are back? If you send a courier now, they can be back here this evening."

As long as he got to spend the night with Annabel as his wife, Thorsten didn't mind waiting a few more hours. "My mother and sister won't be happy about being left out while your family attend."

"Then send a courier to them as well."

"My mother is not in good health, and she needs a large entourage to travel. I doubt she can make it by tonight."

"Nevertheless, you should invite her and let her decide whether she can come or not. She'll be mad at you if you don't."

"That is true."

The cook looked like a heavy weight was lifted off her shoulders. "I need to start preparing for the celebration, my lady." She gathered her skirts and curtsied. "There is much work to do and not enough time."

"Thank you." Annabel turned to the woman and hugged her.

As they left the kitchen, they could hear the cook yelling at her maids to get moving.

"We have letters to write." Annabel smoothed her hand over her hair. "And I need to inform the chief adviser." She sounded as if it was going to be a tough chore.

He pulled her into his arms. "You have nothing to worry about. You parents and everyone else in your court are going to be overjoyed. You marrying the future King of Algenia is the best news they could have hoped for."

16

---

*D*ressed in her mother's wedding gown, and in front of her family, Thorsten's sister, and the rest of the palace staff, Annabel pledged her life to Thorsten and accepted his pledge to her.

Thorsten's mother couldn't make the journey on such short notice, but she'd sent her congratulations, wishing them a happy and fruitful marriage. Evidently, she was too overjoyed that Thorsten had chosen a wife to care about much else.

"You may kiss the bride," the priest said.

To loud applause and cheering, Thorsten did more than that. He lifted her into his arms and climbed the stairs to the second floor. "Your room or mine?"

"Mine. But it's yours now."

As he entered her bedchamber, he kicked the door closed and then lowered her to her feet. "Turn around."

As soon as she did, he started on the row of small buttons at her back.

"I can call a maid to do that."

"From now on, I'll be the only one undressing you."

"What about when you're gone on official business?"

"You'll come with me."

She laughed. "I'm fine with that."

At some point, children would arrive, and she would have to stay behind. But that was a discussion for another day.

With only her chemise covering her body, Thorsten lifted her up and put her on the bed. When she made a move to remove that last piece of clothing, he stopped her. "Let me close the curtains first. Your nude body is a feast for my eyes only."

After plunging the room into near darkness, Thorsten started on the buttons of his own shirt, and Annabel held her breath. Leaning against a stack of pillows, she watched him with hungry eyes. Finally, she was going to see her husband fully naked.

Except, Thorsten turned around as he pushed his pants down, presenting her with his sculpted, muscular buttocks.

Was he suddenly shy?

Impossible. Her Thorsten didn't have any insecurities. He was the most confident man she'd ever met.

Perhaps he didn't want to frighten her?

Annabel had never seen that part of a man's anatomy, not with her eyes, but she'd had her hand on Thorsten's and that gave her a good impression of what his manhood looked like.

When he was done removing everything and turned around, the sight of his proud erection didn't evoke apprehension, only excitement. Imagining Thorsten thrusting that hard length into her, Annabel's inner muscles contracted almost painfully, and she felt herself grow moist between her legs.

"I want to touch you," she said.

He came closer, standing by the side of the bed, his manhood an offering she eagerly accepted.

Flipping to her stomach, she reached for his shaft. Smooth and hot, it was mouthwatering...

Out of nowhere came an impulse to take him into her

mouth. To lick him all around like he'd done to her. Not because she wanted to return the favor, but because she craved it. Experimentally, she extended her tongue and licked the mushroom-shaped top.

Yum. A little salty, a little sweet, all Thorsten.

He groaned, his hips surging forward. "You're killing me, woman."

With her palm stroking him up and down, she cupped his testicles with her other hand and closed her mouth over the mushroom head. It was a mystery where the knowledge of what to do came from. She just knew what would bring him pleasure.

Letting his head fall back on his neck, Thorsten thrust into her stroking hand, but only for a few moments.

Touching her cheek with his fingertips, he gritted, "I'm not going to last like this. I need to pleasure you first."

Reluctantly, she let him pull out of her mouth.

Flipping her around with ease, Thorsten positioned her so she was lying on her back with her legs dangling over the side. He knelt on the floor and lifted them over his shoulders.

"And now I feast." He smacked his lips and dove in.

Annabel tensed for a moment, but apparently, Thorsten was either a quick learner or extremely attuned to her and her body's responses. He remembered exactly how she liked it. His thumbs spreading her labia, his tongue penetrated her entrance, scooping up her juices and then thrusting in and out. When he had his fill, he moved to pay attention to her clit, rimming it but avoiding direct contact.

Pure bliss.

Relaxed, Annabel stretched her arms over her head and surrendered to her husband's expert tonguing. One thick finger breached her tight entrance, slowly, gently, sliding in and out a few times before a second one joined it. The friction was delicious, and combined with what his tongue was doing she was getting close, the tight feeling in her womb increasing with each passing moment. But then a third finger joined, and it was too much. She was too tight down there and the stretching burned.

It was worrisome. Thorsten's three fingers weren't nearly as thick as his manhood. It was going to hurt. But if she wanted to consummate their marriage tonight, she had to let him stretch her in preparation.

He lifted his head. "Okay?"

Annabel nodded, but he was too attuned to her to buy it. "I'm rushing you. I'll slow down." He pulled his fingers out, replacing them once more with his tongue.

As the burning sensation immediately subsided, Annabel sighed in relief.

His fingers dug into her buttocks as he lifted her to his mouth. Ravenous, he alternated between spearing her with his tongue and licking the side walls of her clit. Faster and faster he went, his hungry growls providing the additional vibration that pushed her over the cliff.

As Annabel erupted, Thorsten kept licking and penetrating her with that talented tongue of his, bringing her to yet another climax.

"I want you inside me," she said when the last of the shudders subsided.

"You're not ready."

"Please, Thorsten. I want you. I don't care if it hurts a little. I want us to consummate our marriage and complete our bond."

After a moment of hesitation, he climbed on the bed and pulled her into his arms. Kissing her softly and caressing her everywhere, he murmured, "I'll be as gentle as I can."

"I know you will. And I will not break. What's a little pain in exchange for a lifetime of pleasure?"

She must've been very convincing because he had her under him in a blink of an eye, his thick erection nudging her opening. But he didn't push in. Instead, he kissed her mouth, then trailed kisses down the side of her neck, and then paid attention to her breasts until he got her panting with impatience.

"Please, Thorsten, now."

Rearing to his haunches, he looked at her. "Pull your knees up and spread your thighs for me," he commanded.

Gone was the gentle lover, replaced by the dominant prince. She loved both sides of him, but at that moment she needed the commanding prince, and Thorsten had somehow known that, even though it went against common sense. Normally, a virgin needed to be handled with care, just not this virgin.

To Annabel, Thorsten's dominance was an aphrodisiac.

Just as he'd instructed her yesterday up on that hill, she obeyed immediately, and the look of satisfaction on his face was her reward.

"That's my girl." He ran a finger along her slit. "So wet and ready for me."

Oh, God, she loved it when he talked to her like that. "I am, my prince."

Thorsten leaned over her, bracing his weight on one outstretched arm, and fisted his manhood. Rubbing it against her core, up and down without breaching her entrance, he coated his shaft with her slickness.

When he pushed in, it was only with an inch or two of his length, and then he waited for her to adjust. Oddly, the large shaft lodged inside her stretched her more comfortably than his three fingers had. There was no pain, only fullness and a hunger for more.

"Give me more," she demanded.

He did, pushing in just another inch. "Good?"

She nodded, this time not faking it. It was good. Very good indeed.

"More?" he asked.

"More."

He surged inside her with one powerful thrust, sinking all the way until he hit the end of her channel.

Annabel cried out, more from the pain of him going so deep and bumping against her cervix than from the loss of her virginity.

He stilled inside her.

Joined. They were joined. His presence inside her a most welcome invasion.

She wrapped her arms around him. "I love you, Thorsten. You're mine forever. Now take me."

"I love you more than I thought was possible." He pulled out and surged back in again. Slow at first, then faster and harder, until she was hanging on for dear life, her hands clamped over his buttocks and urging him on.

His shaft getting even harder and thicker, he erupted with a roar, wresting another climax out of her. With her inner muscles convulsing around him, he filled her with jet after jet of his essence.

A few moments later, Thorsten pushed off her so she could suck in a breath and rolled to his side. Kissing her cheek, he pushed her damp hair off her forehead. "I think we've just made a baby."

"I think so too."

"$\mathcal{M}$r. Sorensen, you can open your eyes now."

Who is that guy talking to?

"Samuel, wake up. Your session is over."

With a gasp, Sam's eyes popped open, and he looked around him in stunned disbelief.

"I know, it's weird for the first couple of minutes. But it will all fall into place. What's real and what's virtual will sort itself out."

Holy crap. It was all a fucking simulation. None of it had been real. No, that wasn't true. Somewhere out there was a flesh and blood woman who'd spent those three hours with him.

His perfect Annabel.

Who in his right mind thought that this was fun? Waking from a perfect dream to a much less than perfect reality was like having a bucket of ice dropped on his head.

I'm going to strangle Gregg.

"Ms. Montgomery, wake up. Your session is over."

Session? What was she talking about?

Lisa opened her eyes and looked around the small room with all its sophisticated equipment.

The technician was busy peeling sticky pads off her body, together with the wires that were attached to them. "It's a little confusing for a few moments, but don't worry about it. Your brain will sort everything out. You'll know who you really are and remember who you were in the virtual world."

A virtual world. The man of her dreams, her husband, was a construct of her imagination.

Except, he wasn't.

Somewhere in the world, there was a man who'd played that part.

It had felt so real.

"Can I use the bathroom?" Lisa asked as soon as Sarah removed the last wire.

"Sure. It's over there." The technician pointed to the same bathroom Lisa had used before. The woman was right. Now that the initial confusion was gone, she had no problem distinguishing between the two worlds.

The problem was that she didn't want to.

Rushing to the bathroom on shaky legs, Lisa barely had time to close the door behind her when the tears came rolling down. And then came the sobs.

Such an overwhelming sense of loss. How would she ever get over that?

She felt as if she'd lived an entire other life, and she desperately wanted it back because it was so much better than her real one.

18

*E*ver since her virtual story had ended, Lisa kept checking her incoming emails obsessively. Maybe her Thorsten, whatever his real name was, would request a meeting.

If he'd been as deeply affected as she had, he would. True, she could've been the one to initiate, but she had a good reason for not doing so.

If the real Thorsten was as confident in this world as he was in their shared virtual experience, then he wouldn't hesitate to request a meeting. He wasn't the type of guy who would wait for her to take the first step. Unless he had no wish to find her.

But Sunday had come and gone, and then Monday, and by Tuesday she accepted that the email wasn't coming.

Her dream lover wasn't interested.

It was time she stopped moping around and grieving for a fake life and a fake relationship that existed only in her imagination and the virtual universe of the Perfect Match servers.

"You're scaring me, dude." Gregg walked into Sam's office with a cardboard tray holding two cups of Starbuck's coffee. He pulled one out and put it in front of Sam.

"What do you want?" The coffee was welcome. Gregg wasn't.

"It's seven-thirty in the morning, and you're already here, when I know you were here at least until ten last night because that was when I got an email from you about the Carlton job."

"That's right. You'd better start working on it because they are getting impatient. I promised them we would have their network secure in under a month."

"As soon as Roger's team finishes the Bank of Omaha job, they'll get on it."

"And when is that going to happen?"

"In a day or two. They are wrapping it up."

Sam pushed his fingers through his hair. "I can't keep bringing new jobs if you and your guys can't take care of them. Hire more people if you have to, but get it done."

Gregg removed the lid from his coffee to let it cool. "It's not about the jobs, and you know it. Stop being a stubborn son of a bitch and request a meeting."

His partner was a great guy and a genius at what he did. But humans were not computers, and the logic that made Gregg an outstanding programmer didn't apply to human interactions. Problem was, the guy thought he was great at it.

"It wasn't real. She might be married, or she might be as ugly as sin. I would rather keep the pleasant memory."

"Coward."

"Maybe I am. In either case, it's none of your business. Stop wasting my time and yours and get to work."

Shaking his head, Gregg palmed his coffee cup and walked out.

Good riddance.

19

The long day at the office hadn't helped improve Lisa's mood. And the two extra hours she'd stayed to untangle the mess one of the interns had made of a new client's file hadn't added cheer to her day either.

It was seven o'clock in the evening when she was finally done. Aside from her, the only one still in the office was one of the senior partners. Since his door was open, she felt obligated to say goodbye even though she wasn't in the mood to talk to anyone.

One of the perks of being an accountant was that she could get away with not interacting with people for days at a time. It was the perfect job for an introvert.

"Lisa, what are you still doing here?" Mr. Jacobson asked.

"Untangling some mess. I just wanted to say goodbye before I head out. Do you want me to lock the front door? You're the last one here."

"Thank you, but it won't be necessary. I'm almost done myself. Have a good evening, Lisa."

"You too."

Mr. Jacobson, who was in his early sixties and recently divorced, seemed too happy to be left alone in the office.

Rumors were that he had a fling with someone in the building.

Pressing the button for the elevator, Lisa sighed. Even a pudgy, nearly bald, sixty-something-year-old was having a romantic adventure. In the real world.

How pathetic was it that she was still moping about a virtual one?

The underground parking was going to be deserted this late in the evening, and Lisa wasn't looking forward to walking to her car without a soul around. Patting her purse, she was comforted by the familiar feel of the pepper spray canister she never left home without.

Better safe than sorry was a motto Lisa lived by.

Except, even the safest route, a fling in a virtual fantasy world, had proven to be dangerous and confirmed her belief that nothing and nowhere was really safe.

At least the pepper spray could fend off real-world muggers and rapists. Reaching into her purse to pull it out, she didn't lift her head when the ping announced the elevator, and she was still fishing for it as she stepped inside.

A loud intake of breath alerted Lisa to the fact that she wasn't alone in there, and as she looked up to see who she was sharing the ride with, the purse dropped from her hand.

"I'm so sorry for startling you." Her mystery man crouched down and started collecting the items that had spilled out of her purse.

He looked so much like Thorsten that seeing him felt like a punch to her gut. But then it wasn't a big surprise that he did. When asked to describe her ideal man, she'd been thinking of him.

Straightening, he handed her the purse and offered his hand. "I'm Sam."

"Lisa." She placed her hand in his, half expecting lightning to strike. But all she felt was warmth and an excited flutter in her tummy.

She finally had a name to put with the face.

Sam held on to her hand longer than what was considered polite, but she was loath to pull it away.

"Lisa," he repeated. "I don't know why, but you look more like an Annabel to me."

EPILOGUE

Six years later.

"*M*ommy, tell me the story about the princess who didn't want to marry the prince."

Lisa climbed in bed with her daughter and pulled her against her side. "Aren't you tired of that story? How about I read you one about a different princess?" She reached for one of the books in the stack on top of Sarah's nightstand.

They were all about one princess or another. Sarah refused to listen to any other stories.

"No. I want that one." The five-year-old pouted.

With a smile, Lisa kissed her daughter's warm cheek and decided to elaborate on the story, adding a beginning she'd skipped over before. "It all started one summer when a friend of Annabel's brother came to stay with her family for a month. Thorsten was fifteen, the same age as her older brother, and the most handsome boy she'd ever seen."

"How old was Annabel?"

"She was ten."

"Did she like him?"

"Not at first. She thought he was too full of himself."

"What does it mean?"

"It means that he thought that he was the best, the strongest and most handsome young prince."

"That's because he was." Sam entered their daughter's room and got in bed on her other side. "Continue the story, mommy."

"Yes, Daddy." Lisa winked at him over Sarah's head. "So as I was saying before we were interrupted, Annabel thought that Thorsten was arrogant, which is another word for full of himself."

Sam cleared his throat.

"But pretty soon she realized that he was indeed the best of all princes. The problem was that she wasn't the only one who thought so. Other princesses thought so too. Especially the evil Rowenia." She leaned to whisper in Sarah's ear. "She was a witch, and she cast a spell on Thorsten."

Sarah's eyes widened. "What kind of a spell?"

"To make him choose her as his queen."

"Did she also put a spell on Annabel? Was that why she didn't want to marry him?"

"No. But the spell Rowenia put on Thorsten made him stay away from Annabel, and he didn't come to visit her for many years. Annabel thought he'd forgotten about her. So when the summons to the ball went out to all the princesses, she ignored it and didn't go."

"Was she mad at Thorsten?"

"A little. But mostly she thought he didn't care for her, and she also really didn't want to become queen."

"Why?"

"Because she didn't want to leave her mommy and daddy whom she loved very much."

"But even though Rowenia tried to put another spell on him, Thorsten had never forgotten Annabel," Sam said. "When she didn't come to the ball, he took a horse and rode all the way to her palace. He had to convince Annabel to marry him."

Sarah pursed her lips. "Prince Thorsten wanted to marry Annabel. Was it because Rowenia was an ugly witch?"

"Rowenia was very beautiful," Lisa said. "She was tall and slim and had all the best dresses. But she was mean, and Thorsten saw right through her. He knew she didn't love him and only wanted him for his crown."

"But Annabel really loved him."

"With all her heart." Lisa looked up at Sam and smiled.

"Annabel's love helped break the spell," Sam said. "All Thorsten had to do was to think of the lovely Annabel and no magic in the world could overpower the love he felt for her."

Sarah lifted her eyes to her daddy. "And they lived happily ever after."

He wrapped his arm around her shoulders and pulled her closer to him. "Not right away. Rowenia was so angry when she heard they got married that she cast a spell on Thorsten and Annabel, transporting them to the future where they didn't know each other. They were different people in that new world. They didn't look like they did before and they had different names."

Lisa had never told Sarah that part of the story, but it seemed that Sam found a neat way of bringing the two parts together. The virtual and the real.

"So how did they find each other?" Sarah asked.

Sam kissed his daughter's forehead. "Rowenia was so mean that she thought it would be a great joke to put them in the same office building. She thought that it would be funny if they met in the elevator almost every day and didn't recognize each other."

"Did it work?"

"Of course not," Lisa said. "A love as powerful as theirs couldn't be contained. The first time they met in that elevator, Annabel knew right away that the handsome man in the dark blue suit was her Thorsten."

"And Thorsten knew right away that the pretty dark-haired young lady with glasses was his Annabel."

Sarah turned to look at Lisa. "You have glasses, mommy, and daddy wears suits to work."

"My smart little girl." Sam kissed the top of Sarah's head. "You solved the mystery. In the future, Annabel's name was Lisa, and Thorsten's name was Sam."

Lifting her arms, Sarah wrapped one around Sam's neck and the other around Lisa's, pulling both of them to her cheeks for a sandwich kiss. When they had their fill of smooching their sweet little girl, she chimed happily, "And they all lived happily ever after."

"She's asleep," Sam whispered.

With a soft kiss to their daughter's forehead, he gently lifted her little hand off his chest. Careful not to shake the mattress, he quietly got up and tiptoed out of the room.

Sam didn't go far though. Standing just outside the door, he waited for Lisa to join him. She turned the nightlight on and followed him out.

"Happy anniversary, my love," he said as he pulled her into his arms. "I've planned something special for us this year."

"A vacation?"

Since Sarah's arrival, they hadn't traveled anywhere without her. Both Lisa and Sam couldn't bear the thought of spending more than one day away from their precious little girl. Lisa still wasn't ready, but lately Sam had been talking about her being stressed out and needing time off.

It wasn't easy to balance work with motherhood. Even though Lisa had the best possible babysitter for their child,

Sam's mother, and a crew of four came once a week to clean their house, she felt as if she wasn't doing an adequate job on either front. When at work, she felt guilty for not being with Sarah, and when at home, she felt bad for not putting in the hours necessary to advance her career. Lisa was still only a junior partner in the accounting firm she worked for.

Perhaps that was the reason their attempts to get pregnant again weren't working.

With a smirk, Sam pulled out two blue envelopes from his back pocket. "Since you don't want to leave Sarah behind and go on a real vacation with me, how about a virtual one? We can have several days of adventure crammed into three hours."

Other than the first and only time that had jumpstarted their real-life relationship, they hadn't gone back to Perfect Match. After guessing his virtual princess's real identity, Sam had swept Lisa off her feet in the real world, and they'd been married less than two months later.

"Is Perfect Match doing vacations now? That's brilliant. They can reach a much broader clientele than what they get with just the virtual hookups."

Sam laughed. "I'll suggest that to them, but no. Our vacation is back in our own fairytale land. What say you, princess Annabel?"

Sounded exciting, but also scary.

Now that she knew an entire lifetime could be crammed into three virtual hours, and her real life would be forgotten entirely, Lisa wasn't sure she had the guts to do it again. Also, the thought of forgetting her daughter, even for a few hours, filled her with unease.

"I don't want to forget Sarah."

With a smile, Sam pressed a soft kiss to her lips. "Does our daughter star in all of your dreams?"

"Well, no. Not all of them."

His point proven, Sam looked smug. "Think of it as

taking a long afternoon nap and having a fun dream. Can you live with that?"

"I guess so. Do we get to fill out new questionnaires?"

He narrowed his eyes at her. "Why? Do you want to make changes to our fantasy land?"

"Not changes, but maybe a few little adjustments."

In the real world, she and Samuel had been strictly vanilla, and Lisa was too shy to remind him that his wife was a little kinky. Perhaps Annabel could do that for her.

EXTENDED EPILOGUE

"I have bad news," Thorsten said as he joined Annabel in the palace's courtyard. "A courier just arrived with a message from Rowenia. She is coming for an official visit as her father's representative."

"When?"

"This evening."

"That's very short notice."

His booted foot on the fountain's low enclosure, Thorsten braced his elbow on his thigh and leaned closer to Annabel's ear. "She's plotting something. Nothing Rowenia does is what it seems. She always has a hidden agenda."

Annabel shrugged. "What can she do? We are already married."

The big royal wedding was a month away, but the rumor of their private ceremony had spread like wildfire throughout the known monarchies. Thorsten's bard had composed a poem for their whirlwind marriage, making it sound very romantic and sweet.

It had been a brilliant move, even if unintentional.

The people were enamored with the love story of the childhood sweethearts rekindling their love as adults.

Thorsten's unofficial nickname had changed from a Prince Brute to Prince Charming.

Everyone was happy. Except for Rowenia.

Taking a seat next to her on the fountain's enclosure, Thorsten raked his fingers through his hair. "I don't know what she wants, and that bothers me. I need you by my side when she arrives."

Annabel smirked. "Is the mighty prince afraid of the big bad witch?"

"Terrified."

He wasn't. But if her husband needed her there for moral support, Annabel would face the witch and fight her off him too.

"Then of course, I'll be there." She leaned over and kissed his cheek. "I'll even hold your hand."

"Thank you." He wiped imaginary sweat off his brow.

"But if I'm to face Rowenia, I'd better change into something more impressive." Annabel glanced down at her simple dress and the apron with splatters of paint on it. "I've heard she is very beautiful and elegant."

Hooking a finger under her chin, Thorsten took her lips in a quick kiss. "She can't hold a candle to you."

"You're sweet, and I know that you love me, but I'm not a great beauty by anyone's standards." Annabel cast him a challenging look, curious to see if he'd pick up the gauntlet.

Her belly filled with excited butterflies, she pushed up to her feet, collected her art supplies, and put them in their case.

Since saying anything negative about herself was strictly forbidden by the rules Thorsten had put down for her, and especially in public, that statement would most likely earn Annabel a spanking.

Or at least she hoped it would.

Despite all the posturing he'd done on that hill when he'd come courting, if one could call what he had done courtship, Thorsten still had to make good on his promise. Other than a slight smack here and there during lovemaking, he'd been neglectful in that department.

Following her up, he whispered against her ear. "You're lucky we are not alone. Otherwise, I would've smacked your lovely bottom for talking derisively about my wife."

"Well, your Highness. It seems that you're not being strict enough with your subjects." She winked and turned on her heel.

Not surprisingly, the sound of his boots stomping over the pavers followed her out of the courtyard.

Glancing at him over her shoulder, Annabel pretended innocence. "Are you coming with me to change your clothes as well?"

"Yes." His smile was wicked. "That's exactly why I'm following you to our bedchamber."

"Should I call your manservant?" Annabel teased as she entered their suite of rooms.

"I think we can manage without him." Thorsten closed the door and pulled her by the elbow, turning her around to face him. "What did I tell you would happen if you made self-deprecating comments?"

Annabel's bottom clenched in anticipation. "That you're going to spank me?"

He smiled. "Precisely." His gaze adoring rather than cross, he cupped her cheek. "Have I been neglectful, my love?"

Heat rushed up Annabel's face, but after all the effort she'd put into this, she wasn't going to back out. Lowering her eyes, she murmured, "Someone made some promises he's not keeping."

"I thought you didn't want me to do it ever again."

The heat spread all the way up to her ears. "You know that it turns me on," she said in a barely audible whisper.

He chuckled. "You made such a big fuss about wanting me to promise not to do it again that I thought it was too embarrassing for you."

With a sigh, she leaned her forehead on his chest. "At the time it might have been true. But now that we are married, I don't want any pretense between us."

His hands roaming over her back, Thorsten kissed her. Softly at first, but that didn't last long. After a moment, he gripped her bottom, lifted her up, and carried her to their enormous bed.

Thinking he was going to put her down, Annabel had a brief moment of disappointment. That was not where she wanted to be. Well, eventually, but not right away. But at the last moment, Thorsten turned them around, sat on the bed, and upended her over his knees.

Her cheek resting on the silk bedding, Annabel let out a relieved breath. Finally, she was going to get what she'd been craving for so long.

"Such beautiful legs you have, my love." He gathered the hem of her dress, pulling it up ever so slowly, baring and caressing every inch of exposed skin before pulling it up a little higher. First were her calves, next were her thighs, and when the skirt was all the way up, bunched up around her waist, he bent and kissed the top of each mound over her panties before pulling them down her thighs. "You have the best ass in all the known monarchies and beyond."

Giddy with excitement and somewhat overwhelmed by what was about to happen, Annabel stifled a giggle. Hopefully, it had been a figure of speech, and Thorsten hadn't actually seen them all to make the comparison.

Tucking her closer against his belly with one hand, he covered her entire bottom with his other.

"It's small but perfect." He kneaded one cheek and then moved to the other. "Well, that's enough preamble. Time to administer your punishment, young lady. I think ten spanks would do as a warmup."

Annabel's eyes popped open. Ten? And that was just a warmup?

That was more than he had given her up on that hill.

His hand resting on her bottom, he bent down and nuzzled her neck. "After those ten, you'll tell me if you're up for more. Deal?"

She should've known her Thorsten wouldn't do anything she wasn't ready for. "Deal."

The first smack caught her by surprise, not because of the sting, but because of how loud it was.

She tensed. "The servants will hear."

"There is no one on this floor. I sent them all to scrub the public areas in preparation for Rowenia's visit. But you are right. We need to find a better place for the next time you are in need of a spanking." His hand landed on her other cheek and then kneaded the tiny sting away.

Next time. How exciting. She could dedicate a corner of her wardrobe room for that purpose. It was windowless and well isolated.

How wonderfully wicked it would be to have a secret spanking place.

Annabel smirked into the bedcover. She was such a deviant.

But the fact that she could make redecorating plans while getting a spanking meant that Thorsten was way too gentle with her. Now that she didn't feel scandalized about being draped over his knees with her bare bottom up in the air, it really felt more like patting than spanking.

"And that's ten." Thorsten caressed her warmed up skin. "Ready for more?"

Was she ever. "Yes, please."

"I think fifteen should do."

She nodded. If he continued with such a light hand, that would not be enough either, but there was a limit to what she was willing to say.

"I need words, love."

Taking a deep breath, she closed her eyes, glad that he couldn't see her face. "After the fifteen, ask me again."

Oh, wow. Annabel couldn't believe she'd actually had the guts to say it out loud, and judging by Thorsten's stunned silence, neither could he.

A long moment passed before he finally chuckled. "As you wish, my love."

This time, the first smack wrested a whimper out of her mouth. It stung. Not terribly, but it definitely was the real deal. The second one stung even worse.

By the time she'd counted twelve, Annabel had tears in her eyes, but she was also so turned on that if Thorsten touched her dripping wet center she was sure to orgasm right away. What a mess she must've made on his pants.

The last three were the worst.

Her bottom felt like it was on fire, but that only added fuel to her arousal. A few more smacks and she would climax without any further stimulation.

Gently rubbing her heated behind, Thorsten whispered, "How close are you, love?"

"Very close," she breathed.

Annabel had surprised him. Thorsten knew that submitting to him turned her on, and spanking was the perfect vehicle to transport her to the state of mind which she found most arousing. But it wasn't supposed to be about pain.

Except, it seemed that his Annabel enjoyed a little of it to spice up their lovemaking.

Thorsten wondered whether a few more swats would push her over the edge, but the truth was that he preferred doing it with pleasure rather than pain. In a way, Annabel was pushing his limits more than he was pushing hers.

As he swept a finger along her wet slit, a tremor of desire

ran through her, and she arched up to his touch. Knowing how sensitive she was, he gathered her wetness and spread it around, lubricating both sides of the little bundle of nerves that was so incredibly responsive to even the slightest stimulation.

Her hips rolling from side to side, Annabel whimpered something incoherent, but he didn't need to hear her say it to know what she wanted. Pushing a finger into her moist heat, he thrust it in and out of her slowly, making sure it wasn't enough for her to climax.

He wanted to be inside her when she did.

There was nothing more exquisite than the feel of her inner muscles clamping around his shaft.

"Thorsten," she whimpered again as his finger retracted, leaving her empty and needy.

Lifting her off his lap, he put her face down on the bed, her legs dangling over the side. The four-poster was too tall for her toes to reach the floor, but it was the perfect height for him to enter her from behind.

Her eyes hooded with desire, Annabel gazed at him over her shoulder as he tore his tunic over his head, kicked his boots off, and pulled his pants down. "I can never get enough of feasting my eyes on your magnificent nude body," she husked.

"The feeling is mutual, my love."

She was still wearing her dress with the paint-splattered apron over it, but even though he craved the sight and feel of her bare skin, Thorsten didn't have the patience to undress her. Instead, he hiked her skirt back up, bunching it around her waist and exposing her pinked bottom.

When he surged into her, they both groaned.

"Oh, yes." Annabel arched up.

Gripping her hips, he pulled back and drove into her again, going as deep as he could.

Her bottom must be smarting each time his hips

slapped against it, but given her throaty moans and the fluttering of her inner muscles, she was enjoying every bit of it.

Clawing at the coverlet to anchor herself, Annabel groaned in pleasure with his every forward thrust. The sounds she was making and the sight of his shaft going in and out of her were enough to drive him into a lust induced frenzy.

His fingers digging into her hips, he lifted her bottom to meet his powerful thrusts. As he plunged into her over and over again, he grunted like an animal, but Annabel was right there with him. Lifting to meet him halfway, she was nearly as loud as him.

They were both nearing their peak.

Gritting his teeth, Thorsten waited for Annabel to reach hers first. Only when she screamed, her inner muscles tightening and squeezing around his shaft, did he let go of his tenuous self-control and erupted inside her.

"I love you," he murmured as he wrapped himself around her back, careful not to squash her with his weight.

Except, words weren't enough to express the barrage of feeling that had washed over him. Love, tenderness, gratitude, pleasure, hope—it was a sea of emotion that he was happily drowning in.

"You are my everything, my Annabel."

He allowed himself another moment of holding her tight and then withdrew. "Don't move," he said as the evidence of their lovemaking dripped down her thighs. "I'll bring a washcloth."

Annabel chuckled, which caused more of his essence to pour out of her. "I don't think one would do."

He ended up bringing an entire stack and a bowl of warm water. Tending to his wife after they made love was a task he wasn't willing to give up, no matter how many times Annabel had told him she could do it herself.

Their lovemaking wasn't gentle, and it took a lot out of her. The least he could do was to take care of her after.

When he was done, Thorsten sat on the bad and lifted Annabel into his lap. Cradling her in his arms, he kissed her neck, her cheeks, her eyelids, showering her with the tenderness he couldn't have summoned before.

She sighed contentedly. "I love it when you do that."

"What, this?" He kissed the other side of her neck.

"Yes. It's a sweet side of you that no one but me ever sees." She rested her cheek against his chest. "I'm wiped out. Do I have time for a short nap before the evil witch gets here?"

Damn. He should've thought of that before exhausting her. "You can take as long as you please. I'll deal with Rowenia by myself."

She lifted her head and cast him a mock glare. "If you think I'm going to let you meet with her without me, you are dearly mistaken." She smiled and kissed the underside of his jaw. "I'm very protective of what's mine."

———

Annabel tried her best to give Rowenia the benefit of a doubt, but the woman was even worse than Thorsten's descriptions of her.

"Congratulations on your nuptials," she said while looking Annabel up and down with a fake smile and a thinly veiled distaste.

Plastering a sugary smile on her face, Annabel pretended not to notice. "I'm so glad that you took the time to come and congratulate us in person. You must be a very dear friend of my Thorsten."

For a brief moment, Rowenia gaped at her as if she'd lost her mind, but the woman recovered quickly. "Of course. We've known each other for years. But with our responsibilities as crown prince and princess of our respective monarchies, I'm afraid we didn't have time to nurture our relationship." She cast Thorsten a suggestive glance.

He, in turn, seemed perfectly happy to let Annabel lead the conversation.

Annabel nodded sagely. "I understand perfectly. It's such a big responsibility. The man you will one day wed should be prepared to aid and support you once you become queen, the same way I'm aiding and supporting Thorsten." Annabel leaned forward. "Imagine what would have happened if you had married Thorsten. Where would you have lived? Your monarchies don't even share a border."

Rowenia waved a dismissive hand. "There would have been no need for shared accommodations. We could've visited each other."

"That's not a marriage." Annabel crossed her arms over her chest. "That's an affair at best, and a flimsy political union at worst."

"Not my idea of marriage. That's for sure," Thorsten finally found his voice. "I want my wife to always be by my side." He wrapped his arm around Annabel's shoulders. "When you fall in love, Rowenia, you'll understand what it's like, and then you'll come here and thank me for saving us both from a life of misery. Power and riches are no substitute for loving and being loved."

Conceding defeat, or pretending to, Rowenia nodded. "Perhaps we can forge an alliance in some other way."

Annabel glanced at Thorsten to gauge his reaction. Was he buying it? Was that the end of Rowenia's attempts at meddling?

Leaning, he offered Rowenia his hand. "I'm looking forward to negotiating the terms."

She shook it. "Don't think it will be easy because I'm a woman. I'm a tough negotiator."

A big grin on his handsome face, Thorsten nodded. "I would be a fool to think that."

His answer seemed to satisfy her. "When should we start the negotiations?"

"After the wedding, which I hope you and your father will attend."

"Of course. Will you save a dance for me?"

Thorsten shook his head. "I'll have to respectfully decline. The only one I will ever dance with is my wife."

Dear reader,

Thank you for reading Perfect Match 2: King's Chosen. If you enjoyed the story, I would be grateful if you could write a brief review on Amazon. Every review makes a difference to an author and helps other readers discover the series.

Click here to leave a review

Ready for the next Perfect Match?
PERFECT MATCH: CAPTAIN'S CONQUEST

Working as a Starbucks barista, Alicia fends off flirting all day long, but none of the guys are as charming and sexy as Gregg. His frequent visits are the highlight of her day, but since he's never asked her out, she assumes he's taken. Besides, between a day job and a budding music career, she has no time to start a new relationship.

That is until Gregg makes her an offer she can't refuse—a gift certificate to the virtual fantasy fulfillment service everyone is talking about. As a huge Star Trek fan, Alicia has a perfect match in mind—the captain of the Starship Enterprise.

Also by I. T. Lucas

DARK ALLIANCE
68: DARK ALLIANCE KINDRED SOULS
69: DARK ALLIANCE TURBULENT WATERS

THE CHILDREN OF THE GODS SERIES SETS

BOOKS 1-3: DARK STRANGER TRILOGY—INCLUDES A BONUS SHORT STORY: **THE FATES TAKE A VACATION**

BOOKS 4-6: DARK ENEMY TRILOGY —INCLUDES A BONUS SHORT STORY—**THE FATES' POST-WEDDING CELEBRATION**

BOOKS 7-10: DARK WARRIOR TETRALOGY

BOOKS 11-13: DARK GUARDIAN TRILOGY

BOOKS 14-16: DARK ANGEL TRILOGY

BOOKS 17-19: DARK OPERATIVE TRILOGY

BOOKS 20-22: DARK SURVIVOR TRILOGY

BOOKS 23-25: DARK WIDOW TRILOGY

BOOKS 26-28: DARK DREAM TRILOGY

BOOKS 29-31: DARK PRINCE TRILOGY

BOOKS 32-34: DARK QUEEN TRILOGY

BOOKS 35-37: DARK SPY TRILOGY

BOOKS 38-40: DARK OVERLORD TRILOGY

BOOKS 41-43: DARK CHOICES TRILOGY

BOOKS 44-46: DARK SECRETS TRILOGY

BOOKS 47-49: DARK HAVEN TRILOGY

BOOKS 50-52: DARK POWER TRILOGY

BOOKS 53-55: DARK MEMORIES TRILOGY

BOOKS 56-58: DARK HUNTER TRILOGY

BOOKS 59-61:DARK GOD TRILOGY

BOOKS 62-64: DARK WHISPERS TRILOGY

MEGA SETS
INCLUDE CHARACTER LISTS

THE CHILDREN OF THE GODS: BOOKS 1-6
THE CHILDREN OF THE GODS: BOOKS 6.5-10

**TRY THE CHILDREN OF THE GODS SERIES ON
AUDIBLE**

2 FREE audiobooks with your new Audible subscription!

FOR EXCLUSIVE PEEKS AT UPCOMING RELEASES & A FREE COMPANION BOOK

JOIN MY *VIP CLUB* AND GAIN ACCESS TO THE VIP PORTAL AT
ITLUCAS.COM
CLICK HERE TO JOIN

INCLUDED IN YOUR FREE MEMBERSHIP:

- **FREE** CHILDREN OF THE GODS COMPANION BOOK 1 (INCLUDES PART ONE OF GODDESS'S CHOICE.)
- **FREE** AUDIOBOOK OF GODDESS'S CHOICE BOOK 1 IN THE CHILDREN OF THE GODS ORIGINS SERIES.
- PREVIEW CHAPTERS.
- AND OTHER EXCLUSIVE CONTENT OFFERED ONLY TO MY VIPS.